# The Glass House

# THE
# GLASS
# HOUSE

*A Novella
and Stories by*

## Laura Furman

THE VIKING PRESS  NEW YORK

LIBRARY OF CONGRESS CATALOGING IN PUBLICATION DATA
Furman, Laura.
The glass house, a novella and stories.
I. Title.
PZ4.9865G    [PS3556.U745]    813'.54    79–56282
ISBN 0–670–34179–7

Printed in the United States of America
Set in Palatino

The author would like to thank the New York State Council
on the Arts for a 1976 CAPS grant in fiction. The Yaddo
Corporation has been more than generous in its support during different periods since 1972, and the author is very
grateful.

"Quiet with Belinda" appeared originally in *Fiction*; "Eldo-
rado" in *Houston City Magazine*; "My Father's Car," "Last
Winter," and "The Smallest Loss," in different form, in *The
New Yorker*.

*For My Mother*

Ô nostalgie des lieux qui n'étaient point
assez aimés à l'heure passagère
que je voudrais leur rendre de loin
le geste oublié, l'action supplémentaire!

Ah, nostalgia for places not loved
well enough in the passing hour,
how I long to make good from afar
the forgotten gesture, the additional act.

Rainer Maria Rilke, "Vergers," 41

# Contents

# My Father's Car

When she called, I was reading. It was late and the light from the standing lamp made a circle over me as I lay on the couch. The cat was curled at my feet. A cup of tea was within reach. When I moved to answer the phone, my book fell to the floor.

It was Gerda calling. If my father had married her, she would have been his widow. Instead, she was the dead man's mistress, a friend of the deceased. Gerda told me I had to come to Brewster and take care of my father's car. It had been a month since my father's funeral and she had asked me before. She had been patient, she informed me, and reasonable. "And really, Rosie," she said, "four weeks is enough. The driveway is too full with that car all the time."

I lied and said I was sorry not to have come sooner and it would be no trouble to come in the morning. But I did add, "It's snowing now. I may not be able to get out tomorrow."

"Surely there are snowplows where you live," she said. "The weather report predicts the snow will stop before morning. It will be clear tomorrow."

"The weather report is for you. Three hours southeast. It's different upstate."

"Different?" she said, as if she doubted it, but we discussed it no further. I told her Anton was away on business, so it was a good time for me to drive down. We agreed I would call in the morning when I knew for certain if I would come. We never questioned if I would come at all. As my father's executor, I had no choice, and, though middle-aged mistresses have no legal claims, she had a natural right to tell me to get his car out of her driveway. Besides, there was no one but me to tell.

I am one of seven children, and I am the only one who saw my father in what turned out to be the last ten years of his life. I was nine when my father left my mother and went to live with Gerda. There were four of us then, and I am the oldest. After he left, we continued to live in Pittsfield, and he continued to support us and to pay us occasional brief visits. My mother continued to have his children. I have wondered why he didn't have children with Gerda, if he liked having children so much. Sometimes on those visits one of my brothers would tell him to get out or stay, and demand that he make up his mind. My father always withdrew from those scenes, and, since Mother never said anything, after a time the boys left him alone. He stopped visiting my mother while I was in college; at least I didn't hear about any more visits, so I guess Gerda won the last round.

If my father was in love with her, it wasn't because Gerda was beautiful. Her hair has been gray for as long as I can remember and she has always worn it cropped close. Her features are as definite as stone, her expression as unchanging as a Buddha's. She came to America from Berlin in the thirties. As a child I had trouble understanding her when she spoke to me. On the few occasions I met her, I listened to her accent, not to her words. The other children refused to visit my father at Gerda's, and my father didn't ask more than once.

I made a folder after he died: Father's Estate. The contents are slim: a life-insurance policy, a bill from the funeral home, a will that leaves it to me to distribute his worldly goods among the children. The others didn't want anything, they told me: some one by one, some representing family factions. Two even refused the thousand dollars per child provided by his insurance. All the more for the rest of us, said one brother. Given the situation, I don't suppose any of them could have been expected to act any better, but they didn't try. My husband, Anton, and I took the money, of course. We are rebuilding an old house in Rensselaer County, and the work goes slowly. After two years, we live in three rooms of a twelve-room house. The thousand dollars would pay for a new roof and for repairing the foundation on the north side.

The funeral was in Pittsfield. At the cemetery, Gerda and my mother stayed away from each other. I considered whether I should stand next to Gerda or my mother. In the end, I stood next to Mother, who must have loved him, and I kept my eye on Gerda, who looked tired and small in her black dress. I didn't know my father was even sick until Gerda told me he was dead. His heart attack had surprised her, but Gerda didn't weep, as Mother did. She wouldn't reveal her loss to us, the aliens across the grave.

After the funeral, Mother went right home, and so did Gerda—to her home. The kids, as we still call ourselves, gathered up our husbands, wives, and lovers and trooped off to Friendly's. We took up every booth in the place, and ordered enormous quantities of ice cream. There were the inevitable wisecracks about family reunions and the last sundae. I didn't mind about that or about the laughing. I hadn't cried myself. But when my sister Carol said she was going to blow her entire inheritance on fried clams and a vanilla thick shake, I leaned over and told her to shut up.

After Friendly's, Anton and I drove to Brewster and checked into a motel. I didn't feel like staying in Gerda's guest room while I went through my father's possessions. In two days I disposed of everything except his car. I put aside his cameras and radio for Anton and me. His stereo was half-broken for years, and Gerda said she would be glad to finally give it to the thrift shop. She didn't need anything of his, she told me. They'd maintained separate rooms in her house and shared a common area on the ground floor. I packed my father's clothes into cartons and made four trips to the thrift shop. They promised to send a truck for his desk, which was hideous, and

I kept a nice pine rocker and a cherry side table. The second day, when I went through my father's books, I was surprised at how many there were. We never talked much about books and reading. I kept his complete editions—Keats, Shelley, Wordsworth, and one of Emerson, whom I've never been able to abide. Anton liked the binding.

Now, four weeks after my father's funeral, Anton was in Chicago. He writes for a magazine there and must be away about a month, all told, each year. After Gerda's call, I thought about her and my father, and I wondered if Anton and I were like them. Gerda, for all her European cool, was the one left behind on my father's visits to my mother. Some nights Gerda must have sat alone with a cup of tea and a book; she must have looked up from her book and wondered where my father was and what he was doing. I wondered if Gerda said her good-byes with any more grace or trust than I did.

In the morning, the snow had stopped and it was clear, just as Gerda's weather report had predicted. By six the snowplow had come and gone, and I did what I had to do: put out the cat, turned down the heat, locked the door. I sat in the cold car while the engine warmed up, and watched my cat watching me from the stoop. The house looked finished. It was early April and the snow would soon be gone. Then the flaws in the foundation would be exposed. Meanwhile, I was more pleased than not to be going on a journey, even if the destination was Gerda's.

Route 22 had been plowed and the shoulders were banked with white snow. By the time I was an hour south, the snow had melted into slush. Farmers were out on their tractors and I could see the brown earth they were turning. I stopped once to telephone Gerda, and she told me not to eat lunch, she would feed me. I decided to take the Taconic and then cross over to Putnam County on 84. Route 22 is more direct, but I was sick of looking at towns and houses. In the past two years, Anton and I have done a lot to our house. We made a kitchen from an old woodshed that was about to cave in. We installed Victorian windows on the west side of the living room and stripped the front door. We ripped down all the old plaster and lath, and insulated. We Sheetrocked the walls and now we're taping the seams, room by room, and painting. An old lady had died in the house, and when we moved in, every room but the bedroom in which she died was stuffed with her clothes and postcards, old books, and corncobs.

As I drove, I pictured the house, and I looked in all the windows. I could see myself in one upstairs window and Anton in another. Anton wants a baby. That would make three of us. My mother had children until she was thirty-eight, so that left me nine more years to block the bedroom windows with children's heads. My mother says how happy it makes her to see us having children of our own. I've watched the multiplication of our family with a colder eye, but still I've watched for it.

The house Gerda shared with my father is a gray saltbox, with an addition on either end. I could see at once that the driveway wasn't adequate for both her VW and his Oldsmobile. He liked the size and comfort of the car, though he complained about the cost of fuel. My father was a real-estate broker, and after his retirement two years ago he began to put together a collection of photographs of houses he considered outstanding. An eclectic collection, he called it. He drove all over Westchester and Putnam counties taking the pictures. He kept the backseat strewn with old newspapers he intended to read when he had the time or inclination, and with contact sheets, prints, and empty film cannisters. "Couldn't do this with seven kids," he told me once, and then remembered he was talking to me. It was true, though—seven kids would have squashed the papers and upset the boxes.

The last few times I saw my father we talked mostly about fixing up old houses. He had a good eye for cosmetic detail but he knew nothing about more basic problems. I sat and ground my teeth while he told me how to hire someone to fix plumbing Anton and I struggled to fix ourselves. He felt like a father then, I suppose, and, of course, he only knew as much as I told him. I pretended to be more ignorant than I was when he questioned me about the house, and I did the same when he questioned me about my brothers and sisters. I hated first his eagerness to know and then his arrogance as he criticized people he knew only through my lies and half-truths.

Gerda was standing at the front of the house when I arrived, and she watched as I stepped over a puddle that had formed in the driveway. I lifted my overnight bag so it wouldn't get wet, and regretted that I wasn't staying in a motel. The lane up to her house was all mud. I stayed on the driveway, sidled past the parked cars, and went in by the kitchen door.

Gerda's house is usually immaculate. The kitchen must have been installed in the fifties, and it is lined with matching appliances, Formica counters, and built-in cabinets. It is all aquamarine, except the floor, which is black-and-white linoleum tile. Now every surface in the kitchen was covered with old clothes, some folded into piles, and others lying scattered on the counters and the Formica table. Also on the table was a collection of pipes and belts and worn leather appointment books, the kind my father used.

"Where did all this come from?" I asked Gerda. "I thought I'd finished everything."

"There was more stored away, I discovered. Will you have coffee with your sandwich?" Gerda said. She took my coat and my bag and laid them on the clearest counter. She pushed aside a pile of ties on the table, and when I was seated she put a plate in front of me with a sandwich cut in quarters, two black olives, and a carrot. The sandwich was very cold, and one of the olives was lined with ice. Gerda must have made up the plate the night before, right after her call, sure I would come whatever the weather.

When she had set two cups of coffee on the table, Gerda pulled out a chair and sat down on a stack of dress shirts. "Do you think me both morbid and tasteless to do this cleaning so fast?" she asked. "Some women hang on forever to such clothing."

"Not at all. Why should you keep these things?" I said.

"You mean it is a little soon. But I do it for myself. To have all the closets and the rooms, and space in my house and my driveway. It is over for me, you see, Rosie."

I began to protest, thinking she meant that she, too, was going to die suddenly.

"I mean over with your father," she said. "My own life goes on. So let us finish this as quickly as possible, shall we? I am sorry to drag you away from your charming home and your husband for this task."

"Anton's in Chicago," I told her.

"So you said." She drank her coffee and I thought about the way she said "husband." I thought of my mother and Gerda at the funeral, and how messy those adults had seemed to me when I was a child.

"I have one more thing to ask of you," Gerda said. "Whether you sell the car today or not, I have no desire to see any of your brothers and sisters again. I am now finished with them as well."

"They didn't mean any harm," I said.

"What do I care what a pack of children mean?" she asked.

"I suppose they mean nothing to you at all. You've never liked children."

Gerda looked at me for a moment; then she said, "I try not to like or dislike children, or categories of anything." She paused. "You were the only child who came and saw your father. So you are what I know of having children."

I cleared my throat. "I should start this car business," I said.

Gerda turned and pulled open a drawer in the cabinet behind her. She took out keys and some loose papers—insurance cards and a registration form. "You have the certificate of death with you? Power of attorney? You are right, Rosie. We will be strict now and stick to the business at hand."

There was nothing I could say without saying more than
I wanted to; Gerda left the room and I went about my
business.

The car started with no trouble, and I backed it down the
narrow drive and headed out to the highway. At a self-service
car wash, I used the hose to take the weeks of snow and dirty
rain off the body, and I shined up the hubcaps a bit. The tires
would get dirty driving to the car lots, but I hosed them down
carefully anyway. I used the vacuum on the upholstery and
the carpets, and to clean out the dashboard ashtray. Though
my father gave up drinking several years ago, he never
stopped smoking. There was only his brand in the ashtray, as
far as I could see, and I wondered if he and Gerda had any
friends or went anywhere with them, to the movies or out to
dinner. Most of my friends in the country live in old houses
and are fixing them up. Before we eat at each other's houses,
we walk around looking at a rebuilt wall or at a newly sanded
floor. The houses my father photographed most often are from
the same period, roughly, and must have been in the same
shape at some point. But I have the feeling that those houses
he admired always had money behind them. I think of the
people who live in them as parents, and of Anton and myself
as children. We are doing something different, I like to think.
I noticed one thing as I headed for the used-car lots. Gerda
must have taken my father's prints and contact sheets. She
hadn't mentioned it to me, but the backseat was clean as a
whistle.

By this time it was midafternoon. I passed one place called
A-1 Autos, with plastic flags flying and shiny cars, but the
flags depressed me. I stopped at a quieter showroom. The
building must have been built in the thirties—it had wrap-
around windows, and glass bricks framing the entrance. There
was no one in the showroom. The red indoor-outdoor carpeting was soaked with melted snow. Along the far wall was a
row of desks and in the middle of the floor there was a new
yellow sports car.

I walked past all the desks. There were six of them, and on each desk was a silver-framed photograph. All the salesmen had children. All had wives. On the last desk the picture was of a young wife and there was only one child, an infant. A pipe lay in the ashtray. I turned to leave, and I saw a man about Anton's age standing next to the yellow car. He looked like the best-looking boy in my high-school class. I wondered how long he'd been watching.

"Well, Goldilocks," he said, "picked your bear yet?"

"I guess it's you," I said. "All the others are off."

"They're off in their dens. It's break time," he said, and he walked toward me.

"I hope so—I mean, I hope it's a break for me," I said. "You see—"

"My name's Ron," he said, holding out his hand. I took his hand and shook it briefly. He touched the customer's chair next to the desk with the young wife and baby. "What can we do for you?" he said. "I see you brought in your Oldsmobile."

"It's not actually mine," I said. "It's my father's."

"What can we do for your father, in that case?"

"You can't do very much for him," I said. "He's dead."

"Sorry to hear about your loss."

"Well," I said. "But I'm the executor of the estate. I have to sell the car now."

"We'll see what we can do for you. I'll have to take it for a test drive, you know. Care to come with me?"

I didn't want to go for a ride with him. I wanted him to buy the car—not even drive in it, just take it away. Even though it was almost spring, the days were short and it would soon be dark. I wanted my father there, so I could tell him to take care of his car himself. "Sure, I'll come along," I said, and the two of us went out to the Oldsmobile.

Ron started the car and listened to the engine. He checked the knobs and buttons; the windows went up and down, the wipers side to side, the lights on and off. When we got out on the highway, he accelerated quickly from ten to sixty, then slowed down. "How do you like the car?" I asked.

"It's a pretty good buggy," he said, "but no one wants cars like this anymore, you understand. Or if they want them, they want them new. I'm telling you this straight."

"How much do you think you'd give for it?" I asked.

"We'll have to see. Every car has a different book value, you know."

We pulled up outside the showroom, and he parked the car exactly where it had been. When we were back at his desk, he took a worn yellow book from his jacket pocket. While he was thumbing through the book, I was arranging the sale in my mind—calling Gerda to pick me up, depositing the money in the estate's account.

"Book value is eight-fifty for that year, that model," he said finally. "I'll give you seven."

"Why only seven?" I asked.

"I explained it to you, honey. Let's face it. I'll be lucky to get rid of it at auction. If you were trading it in on one of our new models"—he pointed toward the car in the showroom— "we'd be able to give you full book. How about it? You look like the kind of young lady who could use a nice new car."

"I have a nice new car," I said.

"But wouldn't you like a sports car? Go out roving?"

"I'm married now," I said. "I don't rove." My neck hurt and I wanted something warm to drink.

"Seven-ten," he said. "That's not bad."

"Not good. I'll let you know," I said.

Driving back to Gerda's, I felt like a fool. None of my brothers and sisters cared, and an extra hundred dollars divided five or seven ways was nothing. I had no idea if my father would have cared that his car was being sold for less than top dollar. I stopped in the village at a phone booth, and I dialed the number of Anton's magazine in Chicago. I put the call through person-to-person collect. Whoever answered hadn't heard of Anton, but the operator persisted. Someone who knew him was found, but Anton was gone for the day. Next I tried his hotel. There was no answer in his room either. It was just as well I couldn't reach him, I thought. I would only complain. I would only annoy him.

I got to Gerda's after dark and found her in the living room. There was only one lamp, and Gerda was making a fire. An empty wineglass rested on the mantel. "I'm teaching myself to do this," she said. "He always did it. For too long. Make yourself a drink, Rosie. You look worn out. I am serving you a cold dinner tonight by this fire. Slices of meat and some vegetables."

"That sounds fine," I said, and I poured a Scotch for myself. There was a pair of wing chairs by the fireplace and I settled into one. I watched Gerda as she crouched at the hearth, wadding sheets of newspaper into tight balls and stuffing them below the wrought-iron grate.

"I have to leave early," I said. "I want to get home while it's still morning."

"You'll be driving in the dark."

"Only for a little while. I'm taking Dad's car with me. I'll leave mine out front—if that's O.K. with you. I can get a better deal upstate, I'm sure."

"Is it really worth it to you?" Gerda said. "If you get one hundred or so more and have to drive to this place three times back and forth, what is the profit? Will Anton drive you?"

She turned and looked up at me, and I felt I presented a sorry picture. "I don't know," I said. "How should I know? I resent being cheated."

"Not so unique, but there are worse things. Make me another drink, Rosie, and we will sit together. You make me nervous when I am below you like this."

Gerda struck a match and tossed it on the paper. I went to get her drink, and when I returned we sat in the two wing chairs and watched the fire struggle to catch hold. Once or twice I strained forward to help it along, but I pulled myself back. If Gerda wanted to learn, she could teach herself. I had spent years of my childhood trying to figure out what my father and Gerda did when they were alone together that was so wonderful, or what we did that was so bad that he left us for Gerda. I imagined that he and Gerda ate their dinners at a round table with a tablecloth on it. I pictured them talking, and there was a spread of food we never ate at home. There was wine on the table and candles; sometimes I put in flowers. But always there was conversation. This evening was a shadow of all those evenings I had imagined, and, for all I knew, may have been for Gerda a shadow of the real thing. I leaned against the high back of the chair and listened to Gerda breathing and to the crackle of the fire. She had used unseasoned wood; it would line the chimney with creosote and become a hazard. Another time I would tell her about it. In the meantime, the light of the fire looked fine on her pine furniture and her bare polished floor.

"I wonder if the person who built this house sat and watched the fire like this," I said.

"Perhaps," said Gerda.

"Maybe he sat with his children here. This was originally the kitchen, wasn't it?"

"So I have been told. Perhaps he did sit by this fire with his children. And perhaps he wanted to go, let us say, to London. Or he might have found this fire not to his liking and wished to go north."

"Why would he have wanted to go farther north?" I asked. "There wasn't anything there then."

"That is a reason, Rosie. Every person thinks they know everything. They think they know what is ahead. With your father's death, I am placed here. For the first time in my life, I have no wish for anything beyond this."

"I wonder if I would miss having children," I said.

"I don't," she said, "but our lives are very different. There is nothing left for me to miss. And there is no payback in missing things. I taught myself that lesson a long time ago."

Gerda got up from her chair and moved to a dark corner of the room. When she reappeared in the firelight, she was carrying two folded tray tables. She set up one before her chair and one before mine. "I'll get our plates now," she said. "You get an early start in the morning, whenever you like. But do reconsider. I only want the car out of here. You need not spend so much of your time for that. Sell it quickly. Give it away. It is not important."

"It's important to me," I said. "I'm the one who's executor. I have to do this right."

"Then you must do it," she said. "Do it in whatever way you can. I have no say in this, after all. It is the business your father left to you, not to me."

"That's right," I said, and I thought then of saying that his photographs were my business, too—the most important part, he might have felt. I thought of telling her to stop telling me what I would or should or might do. But probably we wouldn't see each other after the car was sold, and if she wanted the photographs so badly she could have them. Along with the photographs, I would let her have the secret of having taken them and the satisfaction of thinking that I had forgotten them, and neglected my father the way the other children had.

We said good night a little after nine o'clock. I tried Anton's hotel again, but there was no answer in his room. I went to the guest room in what had been my father's end of the house. As I got into bed, I saw that there was no storm window in the guest room. My father wouldn't have allowed that. Perhaps my father had felt sick longer than he let on, and perhaps as far back as the fall he had stopped caring about heat loss in a room used so infrequently.

In the morning, I woke early. I waited until seven-thirty, but when Gerda did not appear I wrote a note telling her I was leaving behind the keys for my own car, and that I would call in a day or so, when I had sold my father's car. I wasn't really so sure of success, but I couldn't go into that in my note. In the kitchen, there were now several cartons stacked neatly, containing his leather appointment books and old clothes. I left all the cartons where they were. I would take care of them next time. For a moment I thought I would keep my father's appointment books, to find out if he and my mother had ever met secretly. If they had, though, he probably wouldn't have recorded it, so I left them where they were.

The farther I traveled from Gerda's, the brighter and clearer the day became. The seat in my father's car was large and comfortable, but I kept flicking the steering wheel right and left to see how much play there was and how much control I had, so the ride wasn't smooth. I stopped at a gas station on the Taconic, and while the oil was being checked I got out and looked at the engine. It had been steam-cleaned recently. The car hadn't been driven since my father's death, so he must have had it cleaned right before his heart attack. I was sorry now I hadn't asked Gerda if he had been having trouble with the engine. I tried to remember if he had said anything to me about wanting to get rid of the car. Maybe there was a leak and he wanted to see where the oil was coming from. He must have had plans for the car. He must not have expected to die so soon.

It had snowed again overnight, and I stopped in town to pick up the *Times* and some coffee. Once I was on the dirt roads nearer home, I felt encouraged. Maybe Anton had been trying to reach me while I was gone, or maybe he had only been out with friends the times I called him. I was only three turns from home when I looked up to see a hill I am fond of. I could see it right through some woods, and I saw an old woman, dressed in black, climbing up the white hill. She was hunched over and she was climbing slowly, as if each step cost her something. People try so hard, I thought, or don't; they still get nowhere. Even if they only try to make the best of their lives, it doesn't matter in the end. People die, like my father, in the middle of the unfinished business of their lives, and there was no reason to think my end would be any different. If Anton was having an affair in Chicago, if we had a child, if I never saw Gerda again, it wouldn't make any difference.

When the next turn came, I looked back at the old woman,

and then I saw she was a cow. I had been tricked by the white-
ness of the snow and the black of her spotted hide. I felt alone
without even the old woman, and I turned away. I drove the
last miles home a little more quickly than I should have, in my
father's car.

# Quiet with Belinda

The first time Edward woke in his brother's house, Belinda was not with him. He looked to the corner of the room where she'd left her suitcase the night before; it was still there. His own luggage lay next to hers—a small duffel bag and a pile of books.

The day before, his brother Harris and his sister-in-law Emily had left with their children for a week on the Vineyard, and they'd left Edward there in Connecticut as caretaker. He had been instructed by Emily not to stay in the main house but in the guesthouse. The floors of the main house were to be oiled by Gretchen, the German maid who came in three days a week. He had also been told that the children's *au pair* girl, also German, was staying behind. "A week off from the kids," Emily said. Between the *au pair*, the maid, and the man who did the lawns, he and Belinda wouldn't have the place as much to themselves as he would have liked, but it was, Edward reminded himself, a free week in the country.

He heard voices in the kitchen. Gretchen might be there, ready to do whatever she was supposed to do to the floors. If she was, they were already discovered having disobeyed Emily's instructions. Edward pulled on his dungarees in a hurry; maybe Emily hadn't told Gretchen where he should be sleeping.

When he went into the kitchen, Edward was surprised to find Belinda and the *au pair* girl sitting at the kitchen table, each with a cup of something hot, talking and laughing. The *au pair* girl had a gap between her front teeth he found unattractive. She was overweight and looked sorry to see him.

"This is Heike," said Belinda. "She comes from a very important village in Germany."

"Oh, no, no. It is not important village. It is only best in certain dancing." She said the word "willage," and they both smiled when she did, Belinda's sparkle and her gap.

"That's important enough," Edward said, just to be agreeable. He hoped Belinda hadn't been indiscreet. The girl got up and began a retreat. Belinda objected, then glanced in Edward's direction. She waved to Heike.

"See you at the pool," she said.

"See you there."

"I didn't know her name was Heike," Edward said.

"I'm not surprised. No one in your family seems to know anything. Do you want me to make eggs for you?"

He accepted the offer and tried to think of something to say to dodge a discussion of his family, but Belinda went on.

"Did you know that every year Emily goes to Germany and picks a girl from the same village? And imports her? The girl's paid nothing. She's a prisoner here. She's terrified of Emily."

Edward thought of Emily. She was single-minded but vague. She never seemed fully in charge of anything, certainly not of his brother.

"Emily was a German major at Radcliffe," he said. "She speaks perfect German."

"So does Heike. I didn't even get to high school and I don't speak German, but you don't see me kidnapping people."

"Come on, Belinda. I'm sure she's treated perfectly decently."

"I'm sure she's not. Anyway," she laughed, "do you know what Emily does when Harris stays in the city overnight?"

"We know what Harris does."

"She stays up all night, wandering around the house, doing all sorts of little projects. Rearranging the furniture. She puts books in categories. The kids wander too. They eat strange foods. Emily thinks peanut butter and honey is all right for them to live on because it's organic. Heike's going to tell me more later."

"I think I'll read on the porch. It's screened in, so it's a way of being inside and outside at the same time. If the screens aren't full of holes."

"Don't go family on me, Edward, just because we're here. I couldn't take it for a week."

"Come here."

"I'm making these eggs for you. Eggs have to be treated tenderly."

"So do I," he said.

"So do I," she echoed.

Edward settled himself on the porch. There was a wicker couch with chintz pillows, and a glass table that took up most of the porch. It had been on his parents' porch at one time. He set his books on the table: *Natural Right and, History, The Godfather, Eleanor and Franklin.* He'd taken Belinda to visit his parents only once, and the visit hadn't been satisfying from anyone's point of view. His father had called Edward the next day to say how beautiful Belinda was and that he, too, had dated such a girl before he met Edward's mother. The glass table had been given to Harris when he was first married; Edward thought that by the time he married it would be too late to get anything for it, all the presents given and taken.

He watched Belinda walk across the lawn and disappear into the garden that lay before the swimming pool. Even Belinda had been married, for five years. She still received letters from her husband which she wouldn't let Edward read. Probably her husband wanted her back. Edward couldn't understand how he could have let her go. As Belinda explained it, she and her husband had been fine together. "I just didn't want to be married anymore. To anyone," she'd told him. Edward didn't believe her. He didn't believe a lot of what Belinda told him. Especially what she said about what she wanted.

"It's slavery," said Belinda in the kitchen that night. "Ten dollars a week spending money and the fare into the city is six. Round trip. Really, and Emily pretends to be such a liberal. Really, Edward."

It was late for the country. The eleven-thirty movie had ended, and the one-o'clock news was fading from Edward's memory. Belinda was heating milk and honey for them. The house smelled of linseed oil, and he could feel his eyelids and nose reacting to the smell. They were trapped in the kitchen and their bedroom off the kitchen, for while they were swimming in the afternoon, Gretchen had come and oiled the living room and dining room floors.

"I get more money from welfare, Edward. Really."

"Oh. Please stop saying *really* to me. I'm not Emily's damn keeper. She's not even a blood relative. Be reasonable, Belinda. Everyone is like that. Everyone's a hypocrite. You can't go around being indignant about it."

"I'm not a hypocrite."

"Of course you are. You're on welfare because you're supposed to be mentally incompetent, and you know and I know you aren't."

"But I was. I convinced them I was and their psychiatrists, and by the time they were through with me, I was." There was a catch in her voice and she turned her back to him.

"Let's not argue about welfare," he said.

"I'm not a hypocrite."

"All right. You're not. Emily is and Heike suffers from it. Can I have my milk and honey now?"

"She was happy in her village before your sister-in-law played Lady Bountiful and took her away. She's indentured for a year. Those kids make fun of her."

"Why?"

"For saying 'willage.' And because she's not pretty. Your family is full of terrible snobs."

"Did she talk to you about this all day?" Edward asked.

"We talked a lot. Until you came to the pool."

"The leper," he said. He and Belinda drank the warm liquid, inhaling its sweetness. He felt comfortably sorry for himself, remembering Heike leaving the kitchen and then the pool when he'd appeared.

"How's the book you're reading?" she asked.

"Interesting enough. I may be able to finish it tomorrow."

"She was happy in her willage. No one's happy almost any-where."

"Emily's done it for years, Belinda. And some of them aren't miserable. Like Gretchen. She worked for a year and now she's married. A U.S. citizen. Munchkins of her own."

"I'll make tempura for you tomorrow, Edward. Would you like that? I'll make the best meal we've ever had, and it won't cost a penny. The garden's full of food."

Edward smiled at her offer. He preferred cheeseburgers, but he appreciated any gesture Belinda made toward him. As they were going into the bedroom, she turned to him and said, "It must have killed her to leave it right now."

"Who?" He started to caress her.

"Emily," she replied, her voice muffled by his body. "The garden's at its best right now."

Late the next afternoon Edward looked through the screened porch and saw Belinda and Heike walking to the guesthouse. He was almost finished with the next-to-the-last chapter in his book when he saw Belinda coming from the garden with a basket over her arm. He could tell from the way she walked that the basket held something heavy and that she was trying not to show the strain of carrying it. He heard the two women in the kitchen, the sound of pots and knives, then smelled the oil heating for tempura. He gave up his book for the day.

Heike smiled at him when he came into the kitchen. She got off the stool she'd been sitting on near Belinda and, almost with a curtsy, left the kitchen. Edward was slightly offended she'd left that quickly, and he was relieved to be alone with Belinda. She accepted a small kiss on the back of her neck, but she didn't greet him. She was concentrating on slicing the vegetables, and Edward knew she'd set herself a goal—the straightest cut into the only perfect zucchini ever picked.

He opened a beer, hoping the pop of the can would get her attention. It didn't, and he leaned against the doorjamb and watched Belinda at work. She was eccentric, there was no denying that, but Edward thought he was probably in love with her. He wanted more days like this, quiet with Belinda. He wanted to live with her. She was beautiful. Even seeing her every day, he couldn't forget that she was beautiful. This sort of domesticity had been missing too long from his life. He was happy at that moment even for the girl Heike, who provided them conversation, and Edward resolved to give more to Belinda, to be less defensive about his family. He would ask Belinda soon to live with him. Everything would smooth out between them.

"I think she's a lunatic," Belinda said.

"Heike?"

"She keeps frozen tins of mold in the guesthouse. In the freezer." She looked at Edward significantly.

"What a strange thing to do," he said.

"The upper classes go mad. My mother's family did."

"I didn't realize she was upper class."

"You're the one who told me," Belinda said. "Famous old family. Manufacturers of doorknobs or toilet seats. Aristocrats."

She continued slicing until Edward said, "Your mother?"

"No. Not my mother. Not Heike. *Emily*."

"I don't believe it. Why would anyone keep tin cans full of mold?"

"She believes food improves in nutritional value as it rots." She paused to let the word sink in. "She tries to feed it to the kids, but they won't eat it."

"No wonder they prefer peanut butter," Edward said. He didn't believe her, but he didn't want to argue about it. "When will dinner be ready?" He crushed the empty beer can and tossed it across the room to the open waste pail.

"Half an hour. No more. When tempura happens, it happens."

Edward walked toward the pool as if he were going for a swim, but he swerved and ducked into the guesthouse, hoping Belinda hadn't seen him. The house was dark and had a derelict air. As he walked into the kitchen, he noticed an old Pennsylvania chest he'd always liked; his mother had given that to Emily also. Just as Belinda had said, the guesthouse freezer was filled with tins containing what looked like frozen mold. He closed the freezer door and left the guesthouse quickly.

Edward didn't go straight back to the kitchen but into the cellar of the main house. From the nearest rack, he selected a *blanc de blanc* that didn't look too precious, and he went upstairs. He expected to find the table set, the meal ready; instead, as he reached the top of the stairs, he saw Belinda weeping, her head down on the counter. The oil no longer crackled in the pan, and the raw vegetables lay wilting on a paper towel.

"What is it? What's wrong?" He set the wine down on the chopping block and tried to raise Belinda's head. She continued to sob, and he couldn't move her. Finally, she said, "I lost it. My only gift," and she raised her wrist to his eyes. "It's gone," she said.

"What's gone, sweetie?"

"The bracelet my husband gave me. I deserved to lose it, Edward. When he gave it to me, I asked him how much he paid for it, and when he told me," she paused and wiped her eyes and nose, "I told him he'd been taken. Paid too much. Oh, what difference did it make?"

"What did the bracelet look like?" Edward asked.

"Gold chains and opals. I've worn it practically every day. Every time you've seen me. How could you not notice it?"

"We'll retrace your steps," he said. "I'll find it, Belinda."

"It's gone," she said, "and was meant to be gone. I've never lost it before and this means something."

She fell asleep right after dinner, leaving Edward alone in front of the TV. He tried to enjoy the comedy he watched every Saturday night, but it was gloomy without Belinda. He left the house and walked toward the guesthouse. He kept his eyes down, searching the lawn for the bracelet. He walked to the pool and turned on the lights. The bracelet was not in the pool, not trapped in the filter. Edward ran his hand over the lawn, making his way around the pool on his hands and knees, but the bracelet wasn't there. He turned off the pool lights and went into the guesthouse.

Only the overhead light in the kitchen worked and so, in the dark, Edward crawled through the upstairs, feeling under beds and chairs and desks. He found a bottle cap and a fake pearl earring. Downstairs again he searched the kitchen, every cabinet and along the baseboard heaters; even in the refrigerator among the tins of mold. It occurred to him that Heike might have taken the bracelet, but he decided not to mention that yet to Belinda. He turned out the light, having accepted her loss and his failure, when he took a last look behind the Pennsylvania chest. The bracelet was there. The opals shone in the dark like faint moons. He stood there holding it with both hands as though it could escape, and Edward thought of the husband he'd never met giving the bracelet to Belinda.

She was sleeping so soundly when he returned to the main house that Edward decided not to wake her, but to surprise her with the bracelet in the morning. When he handed her the bracelet, however, she only took it. She didn't smile as he'd expected her to do. She looked at the bracelet with red-rimmed eyes. She'd cried herself to sleep, she told him. "I took it as a sign my marriage was really over. I'd accepted that it was gone." She draped the bracelet over her left wrist and closed the clasp. Then Belinda went into the kitchen to start breakfast, and Edward was left sitting on the unmade bed, feeling like a fool.

He wanted to take her out to dinner that night, but she asked if they couldn't stay home. She made cheeseburgers, and they played checkers in front of the TV. She told him, "Thank you for finding the bracelet, Edward. I'd forgotten to thank you," and they let the subject drop. They drank a six-pack of beer between them, and as Edward was about to fall asleep, Belinda challenged him to a game of croquet by moonlight. They laid out the wickets in an irregular pattern that was almost impossible to see; that was the challenge, Belinda said. "Anyone can play in daylight." Just as Edward thought he was getting the hang of it, he tripped over a wicket and he stayed down. He rubbed his elbow and felt the damp night grass soaking his dungarees. Belinda crouched by him and massaged his shoulders, to distract the pain, she said. "It's Heike's day off tomorrow," said Belinda. "Would you drive her to the station? It would save her the taxi fare."

"She could hitch," Edward replied. Belinda took her hands from his shoulders. "O.K.," he said. "O.K., I'll do it. But I ask one thing. When Heike takes her day off, let's take a day off from Heike."

The next morning the three of them got into his car and Edward drove them to the station. Heike was wearing a wool suit and carried a small suitcase and a red hatbox with her. As the train pulled away, she tried to open the window to wave at them, but the window stuck. She knocked on the glass and smiled. Belinda and Edward stood watching until the train was completely out of sight.

"Isn't it a little strange to take two bags to New York for a day off?" Edward asked.

Belinda linked her arm through his and suggested they walk around town.

They strolled past the small health-food store and a store that sold Indian clothing. They looked in the window of the sporting-goods shop at the guns and bows and arrows. Edward felt that their time together was just beginning. As they paused in front of the shop that sold Shetland sweaters and plaid skirts for back to school, Belinda told Edward about Heike's village—dance contests, trips the young people took together to Munich, gymnastics classes—until Edward agreed with her that it sounded like a good life. "Too bad she came here with Emily," he said, "but the offer must have looked good to her at some point. The year will be over in a few months. She'll be the talk of her village—a year in Connecticut."

"A few months!" Belinda spoke so fiercely that he pulled away from her. "You say it so easily and to another person, it's forever."

"All right, Belinda," he said. "But that's all I can do. I'm another person too, you know."

They walked back to the car on opposite sides of the street and didn't speak the whole drive back to the house. When they pulled up at the house, Belinda leaned over and gave him a kiss. "It's all right, Edward. Don't look so worried."

For the rest of the day, they stayed together by the pool. He read *The Godfather* and she practiced diving. Edward took a few breaks and swam in slow full circles around the pool. He wondered how to get Belinda to move in with him. He didn't know how to start talking with her and couldn't really imagine her leaving her own apartment for his; he could see them living together but not how they would get there.

When he finished his book, he looked up and Belinda was gone. He called her name but she didn't answer. He walked toward the garden, calling her again. When he was almost at the garden gate, he saw Gretchen's car pull up. As far as he could remember, she wasn't supposed to come that day, but he assumed she had orders from Emily.

Belinda was bending over a row of lettuce, a pile of dead weeds by her side.

"Gretchen's here," he said.

"Then let's not go into the house until she's gone."

"Didn't you hear me calling you?" he asked.

"I did. But I didn't have anything to answer."

The sun was hot, and Edward walked through the garden. She showed him the carrots, too crowded, and the cabbages, eaten by worms. As she was showing him how zucchini grows from yellow flowers, Gretchen came into the garden. Unlike Heike, he thought, she was an example of German beauty, but a little hefty.

"Excuse me," she said, "but I have news of Heike."

"Does she need a lift from the station?" Edward asked.

"Heike returned to Germany. She called me from the airport as she waited for the plane." Gretchen paused and looked at Edward. "There is a letter for Mrs. Wilde. I left it in the kitchen for her arrival."

"But how did she get money for the ticket?" Edward asked. It was the third time he'd asked the question; they'd discussed it in the garden and then returned to the house. Belinda had made a roast chicken, and they were drinking another bottle of Harris's wine. "And how did she know which plane to take?"

"All right. I'll tell you." He'd thought his questions were rhetorical, but he listened to Belinda. "One day in the garden she showed me the airline ticket. It was the other half of the ticket that got her here. It was valid for a year so I told her she could go. She hadn't known she could use the ticket without Emily telling the government it was all right."

"Do you have any idea what you've done, Belinda? Emily will think I drove her away. This isn't as simple as you think."

"You did drive her away," Belinda said. "Straight to the station."

"No. Because I'm sleeping in the damn house instead of the guesthouse. Or because I'm sloppy. You don't know my family."

"I'm here, too, Edward. And I'm not sloppy."

"They won't know that."

"They'll know I'm here all right. Gretchen is a spy. She wouldn't meet my eyes in the garden."

"She was too busy giving me the once-over."

"No. Servants aren't supposed to exchange glances. Not in front of the family."

"Belinda. Please. You know I love you. You're not a servant."

"I know that," she said quietly.

"And I know it. Dammit, Belinda. I want you to move into my apartment." He'd said it wrong. He saw his empty, dirty apartment just as he'd left it, and he knew he'd said it wrong.

"Heike left," Belinda said, "because she couldn't stand being so lonely. No one had talked to her like a human being in six months. She was afraid Emily would have her put in prison if she tried to escape."

"That's absurd. I don't want to talk about her."

"I do. I could never live with you, Edward. You're ashamed of me and you don't even know it. You feel shame when I talk to servants. You want me to cook for you and sleep with you . . ."

"I said I wanted you to *live* with me."

". . . and you haven't listened to a word I've said about my marriage. I don't want to live with anybody. So don't look so sad, Edward."

"Of course I look sad. I want you. . . ."

"You have me," Belinda said. "Enough of me. As much as you really want."

Edward lifted his wineglass, one of a cut-crystal set of his grandmother's, another gift to Emily, and wanted to grind it into the floor. But he spotted an envelope on the kitchen counter. Emily's name was printed on it in awkward block letters.

He set the glass on the table, spilling some of the wine, went over to the counter, and opened the envelope.

He smiled at the contents and looked at Belinda.

"It's from your little friend Heike, all right," he said. "And you can't read it."

"Why not?" asked Belinda. "Of course I can."

She stood and walked over to Edward, her arm outstretched for the letter. But he held it over his head and with his other arm gripped her shoulder and held her away from him.

"Let go of me," she said, straining and reaching for the letter. "Edward. Let me have it."

"You can't have it," he said, "and you can't read it."

"Of course I can, of course."

"No, you can't," said Edward softly, and he dug his fingers deeper into her shoulder. He said, "You can't read it because it's in German. That's all. That's why. And you don't know German, Belinda."

# Last Winter

In college Annie was a psychology major, and she married a fool. I was in literature and married a junkie. After college, we lived in New York. We met for lunch sometimes, Annie and I, and our slight friendship has lasted longer and certainly proved more pleasant than the associations we formed with our husbands. Pleasant, if distant, but that's the way I've been keeping things lately. Two years ago, when I got divorced, I moved to a farm, an hour from Canada. Most old friends are impressed with that and say how far north I am. But it is just where I live, not north. I could have ended anywhere when I left the city.

Last January I went to New York on business. I edit books free-lance for the publishing house where I worked when I was married. My friend Channing is the house editor I work with most often, and she likes to see me when I finish a project, so, grumbling, worried that I'll bring the wrong clothes, I gather myself up and take the bus to New York. This time I was pleased to be going to the city. Christmas was over and all I could see ahead was long weeks of snow and then rain.

Annie had extended an invitation when she'd visited me in the fall with her friend Patrick and his four-year-old daughter, Cherie. "I have plenty of room," she'd said. "You know that, Ellen. Anytime. Call first."

When I did call, she said that it was fine for me to come and leave my things but that she needed the apartment alone the first night I planned to be in the city because Patrick was staying over. That was O.K. with me. For that one night I could stay with Channing or someone from the office.

Annie lives in the Village, in a building that you enter by walking through a tunnel under another building and across a courtyard. Then you go down some stairs, up two flights, and you are at Annie's door. On the first floor of the apartment there is a small entrance hall, a bedroom, and a bathroom. Upstairs there is a tiny kitchen and a large living room with a marble fireplace and a cathedral ceiling that is two stories high. A skylight runs the length of the room. The walls are painted white and plants hang from the skylight. This room is one of the most dramatic I've seen. It looks like New York to me.

I arrived at Annie's apartment early on a Monday morning, nine hours after I'd left home, and Annie told me she could talk for only a few minutes. She was studying hard for the Graduate Records, she said. Annie had a master's in social work and worked part time as a therapist in a clinic in Brooklyn, but she wanted a Ph.D. in psychology, and was explaining why when the phone rang upstairs. Annie went to answer it, and I settled in, hanging my skirt and my good blouse in the bedroom closet.

After a while, Annie came back downstairs. She leaned against the bedroom door and watched me rummage in my suitcase. "You can sleep here tonight after all," she said. "Patrick's not coming."

"It's off again?" I said.

"Who knows?" She moved into the room and sat down on the double bed. "I never know. He never knows. I'm beginning not to care, I guess."

"How was it over Christmas?" I asked. I hardly knew Patrick. I'd only seen him for a few hours at my house, but I remembered her saying that he went a little crazy on holidays.

"We stayed with my father, and I was so crazy he didn't

get his chance," Annie said. "And we had Cherie with us." She looked up at her bulletin board where, pinned among invitations to art openings and postcards from exotic places, there was a color photo of Patrick's little girl. She was as blond as Annie. She looked like Annie. "It's funny. It's worse for me not seeing her than Patrick," Annie said.

I had troubles of my own. I'd made a date for that night with my ex-husband, Harry, who had written at Christmas to ask if we could have dinner the next time I came to Gotham, as he called it. Since the divorce, we hadn't seen each other. I'd heard he was living with a woman I'd met years ago at a party. She was so drunk she almost fell into the fireplace. Fortunately, it was June and there was no danger. She carried it off nicely.

I'd sent Harry a postcard agreeing to have dinner, because I figured I might never see him again. He'd promised to die young and was now thirty. Either that promise would be added to the others he'd broken or it would happen. I would see him, I told myself, just to check it out.

I told Annie I'd be back about ten. We arranged to have dinner together the following night. I said I would cook. She gave me her extra set of keys, and I watched her climb the stairs back to her books.

Around noon I took the subway uptown and went to the office, where I was welcomed by all my old friends. We sat in Channing's office and talked the usual talk: Life in the city, life in the country. The bottom line, I wanted to tell them, is that it's possible to move great distances and change nothing but the scenery. But I didn't. Instead, I talked cost and climate, views and living without first-run movies. I enjoyed sitting in that glass tower, and I was struck by our confidence that it wouldn't fall or burn as we drank coffee and made jokes. The building wasn't much more than five years old and perhaps when it was thirty would be destroyed and a different one erected in its place.

At some point, six or seven of us were talking and someone,

I think it was Bill from Production, mentioned a salesman named Dieter. He said, "Oh, I knew there was something new to tell you. Dieter is dead." Of course, he wasn't so wrong to be casual. It was old news to him. And Dieter and I hadn't been great or close friends. I'd liked him. We'd had lunch once a week or so and gossiped about people in the office.

"How did he die?" I asked.

"Downtown. On the docks," Channing said. I could tell from the way she said it that she didn't want to keep talking about Dieter; her desk used to be next to mine and we'd listened to each other's phone calls for years.

"What do you mean, the docks?" I said.

"He was beaten to death," she said. "He was gay. You know that."

Poor Dieter, I thought as Channing and Bill discussed Chinese food versus the nearest bar. When I first left the city, I'd been afraid to return and find things had changed without me, and here was Dieter dead, wiped out, simple as that.

We all went downstairs for a long Chinese lunch, then dragged ourselves back to the office and scattered to our places: desks in the hall for proofreaders, copy editors, and secretaries; cubicles with windows for editors. They had adjusted to my being there and it was like old times. I showed Channing what I'd done with my last book, and she gave me a new project. It was by two young architects, tentatively titled "How to Design Anything." I was to meet the authors the next day. They didn't want the book to be too organized, Channing told me, and I was supposed to explain to them that it had to have a beginning, middle, and end.

The day was drawing to a close. I figured I could meet Harry at seven for dinner and still join some people from work at the bar where we used to go. That way, I could be back at Annie's at ten and asleep not long after my usual hour.

At four I called Harry. I could hear him smiling as he said hello to me. Harry is so cold that when he is even cordial it's like the sun. I stood with my back to the group of secretaries' desks and watched the digital clock on the Newsweek Building. Harry and I have always been great phone talkers, and now he began describing in detail his cat's progress across the living-room floor. Finally, I said, "I'd better get off the phone, Harry. How about seven at O'Hoolihan's? I'm going there with Pat and Betsy."

"Seven's a little tight."

"How could it be tight? We're not just going to grab a hot dog for dinner, are we?" I was feeling a little nostalgic now for the days of living with a speed freak—the arguments over whether he would eat or not. I thought I'd hold off telling him about Dieter until we were face to face. He'd liked Dieter the few times they'd met.

"Dinner at all is a little tight," Harry said. "I got a ticket for the opera tonight. *Boris Godunov.*"

"One ticket?"

"I was really lucky to get any. A friend handed it to me an hour ago. It's in the third row. Center."

"Harry. We were going to have dinner tonight. I haven't seen you for years. You haven't seen me. This was your idea."

"Darling. Don't be silly. We can have a drink. If you get in a cab, you can be here in ten minutes, you know. Or we can meet after the opera."

I saw that he thought he was beng flexible, and knew all was lost. "O.K., Harry," I said. "I'll be there."

I hung up and went to see Channing. I asked her if we could go over the manuscript in the morning. "I've got to go now," I said.

She looked at me calmly and said, "Sure. What's the matter? The reprobate again?"

"How did you know?"

"Your hands are a dead giveaway. He can get you shaking faster than anyone."

"Channing, am I unreasonable? We were supposed to have dinner, but someone gave him a free ticket for the opera."

"I don't know about you, but if someone says to me we're having dinner, that's what I assume we'll do. There are not two meanings to that statement."

She spoke so positively that I picked up the phone and dialed Harry's number.

"I can't do it, Harry," I said. "I just rode on a bus for nine hours and worked all day, and I'm not jumping into any cab to see you for fifteen minutes."

"There's more than fifteen minutes before the opera."

"Stop it," I said. "We were supposed to have dinner and now we won't. You stood me up."

"Your self-righteousness astounds me." He paused. "You act as if you never change your plans. I can think of plenty of plans you've changed."

"I don't like the level of this conversation," I said.

"You don't like hearing yourself criticized. That's what you don't like."

"This isn't criticism. This is a sidetrack," I said, and saw that everyone within ten feet was staring at me. It was just like old times, me shouting at Harry over the office phone.

After a silence, he said, "O.K. O.K. We'll meet after the opera. Then we can talk. If that's what you want."

"Harry. That is no concession. And no, Harry, I don't think I want to see you." I hung up.

I had hung up on Harry once before, years before. We were supposed to go on a fishing trip and didn't because at the last minute he called me at work to say someone had invited us to Connecticut—some rich person who was going to lend him money. We'd stay in a mansion, he said; we'd eat pie in the sky. I remembered how hurt he'd been at my not giving him a chance to explain and the fight we'd had that night when I came home. Then I remembered how I felt in the country when I got his letter asking me if I would see him in Gotham and how pleased I had been, and I thought back further to times when we had been the best of friends to one another. I walked into an empty cubicle and dialed Harry's number again.

"I don't like being hung up on," he said.

"That's why I'm calling back," I said. "I'm sorry. I don't like not seeing you tonight."

"We can see each other. I told you."

"Can you give this a little distance for a minute? Can you see my point of view at all?" I was speaking softly, because he also hates being yelled at.

"We can see each other after the opera. Or you can come up now."

"Will you answer my questions?"

"No. You're being completely unreasonable. And you know it. Why do you have to be so emotional about this?"

I hate being told I am unreasonable or emotional, and Harry knows it. "That's it," I said. "There's nothing else to say."

"Of course there is," Harry said, but his voice faded as I took the receiver from my ear and placed it back in its cradle. I sat at the desk for a while and watched people hurry by. Phones rang frantically. Typewriters clattered. How could I have been so stupid and let this happen to me again? I put my head down on the desk and cried.

Channing came over, and Pat and Betsy, my old pals. Bill from Production walked by, I think. I stopped crying. Only exhaustion, I explained, because there wasn't anything left to say about Harry and me.

I went to O'Hoolihan's with Pat and Betsy. Channing came along also, I think to keep an eye on me. She views everyone as incompetent and in need of her cool services to one degree or another. In this case, she was right.

I started my third Scotch and Channing insisted I eat a hamburger. I hadn't eaten beef for months—not since I was last in New York—but I didn't have it in me to explain that to her, to go through the whole conversation. She would think I was an ass, pouring liquor down my throat and talking about my health. I ate the hamburger, which was excellent and rare, and ordered another drink.

We spoke of divorce, of therapy, and then of ex-lovers. Betsy had recently divested herself of one of the best-looking men any of us had ever seen. An orphan, an actor, a baby, a psychotic, she pronounced; but the pride in her voice as she described his antics was a remnant of her feeling for him, or at least of her enchantment.

Pat was more or less living with a man. He was away a great deal, and when he returned she came into the office with great circles under her eyes. They drank, she confessed, until they could hardly see each other and made love until they didn't want to anymore, and then he left. It didn't sound all that bad, but it didn't seem enviable.

They asked me what I did up there in the sticks, and I shrugged, examined the table, and said that I did what I could. In truth, I do very little. Any lover who comes too close looks like Harry, and the others break my heart in a different way.

Only Channing had what could be called a sensible relationship with a man. For four years she has been attending classes in theosophy. At one class she met a man who was also interested in theosophy, and a year later he moved into her apartment. They bicycle together around Central Park. Last summer they visited me on their way to climb some peak in the Adirondacks. But even Channing has something unsettling to say—a thread to add to the ragged day. A few nights before, while they were making love, she'd announced she was bored. What ensued she didn't describe, and we didn't pursue it.

Annie had warned me not to rely on the bell because more often than not it didn't work. She also told me that the building had been robbed four times in the last year and that people always tried to jimmy the lock. Therefore, the set of keys she'd given me might not work. The one for the first door, the door to the tunnel, didn't. I stood there, trying it forcefully and softly, casually and with tension. I thought of Dieter being beaten to death only a few blocks west of where I stood. My fear of being attacked from behind increased until, just when I'd given up, the key turned and I walked through the tunnel to Annie's building.

Annie was upstairs in the big room, sitting on a hard chair before a round dining table strewn with papers and books. The lamp that hung over the table illuminated her blond hair, making it shine. She smiled when I reached the top of the stairs and stumbled on the last step.

"Did you and Harry have a few?" she asked.

"Me and Harry?" I said, not remembering for a minute what she was talking about. "Oh, we didn't go anywhere. Coffee? Tea? I'll make tea."

I stood in the narrow kitchen as steadily as I could and waited for the water to boil, shouting out to Annie how it had really gone with Harry.

We sat with our cups of tea in front of her cold fireplace and Annie talked about her determination to get her doctorate. There was a trust fund, she said. At twelve she had been told she would inherit enough money so that she would never have to work for a living, but she had renounced her money except for a small income. There was an unbreakable clause in the trust, however, which guaranteed her education for as many degrees as she liked—and she seemed to like having several. She could sue now for control of her money, but she would not. At the age of thirty, Annie was content to be governed by a twelve-year-old's sense of the way money should righteously be spent.

Then we talked about Patrick, to whom she'd spoken again. It was hopeless, she said. "He's a child, I'm a child. But he's mad."

Later Annie and I got into long flannel nightgowns and lay side by side in her bed.

"I didn't know it would be like this," I remember saying, thinking how I had viewed thirty at eighteen. I was glad to be at Annie's. I've always liked sleepovers. I was telling her a story about the country—how I was snowed in and didn't mind at first, then did; who came to plow me out—when we both fell asleep.

Annie left for the clinic early the next morning, even before I had to consider getting up and seeing the architects and

Channing. She slammed the door and I heard the police lock snap into place, then silence. I went back to sleep, stretching out on the bed that was now all mine, and dreamed of an old boyfriend and his three brothers. In my dream the boyfriend and I were so in love that it hurt. The brothers floated through the dream like page boys, handing us things, helping us into rooms and through doors.

I opened my eyes, maybe at some slight sound, and saw a very young woman standing in front of Annie's dresser. She was wearing a tan duffel coat. Her hair was blond, but a deeper, pinker shade than Annie's, and she looked no more than twenty. She turned and looked at me, then raised one finger to her lips. Her gesture was a command. Do not look, it said. Do not speak. Close your eyes. Do not be here.

I closed my eyes. The apartment was being robbed. I could be hurt. It was as if I had lost my body below my neck. I could not feel my legs or arms; all I felt, really, were my eyes, closed as commanded. In the darkness there were blocks of light passing. I thought at one point I saw the room again and was afraid my eyes had opened involuntarily.

I considered running for the door, but what would I do outside the apartment, barefoot in my flannel nightgown? I wondered if I was a fool, lying and waiting to be spared. Then I thought, Should I fight? But what for? The credit cards that lay in my wallet on Annie's dresser? Annie's television or stereo?

Then I knew—I don't know how, but I was sure—that she would be joined by a man. I thought of the door again and running. A woman might spare me, but a man would not. I could promise not to tell anyone that I'd seen her, but we weren't children. My promise would mean nothing to them.

I heard the woman go into the little hall by the apartment door, and then she came back into the bedroom and stopped by my side of the bed. There was nothing of value on the night table—my cheap watch, a ring with a glass stone that looks like amethyst, and a paperback book. It was excruciating, trying to breathe evenly as she stood over me. Then she walked away, and there was a certain coldness next to me where she had been. I heard her footsteps on the stairs. My eyes were closed, though she was upstairs and couldn't see me. A long time seemed to pass. I heard the ticking of my watch. From the bathroom I heard a baby crying and then the flapping of wings, and I felt a rush of air. A bird flew through the room and it was over. I opened my eyes.

The first thing I saw was the apartment door. It was closed and the police lock was on. Its bar was in place, braced between the door and the floor. There was no way the woman could have entered the apartment. I got out of bed and dressed quickly. Whatever had happened, I had to be uptown at work. But I was still too frightened to simply leave. I went upstairs and looked around the living room and the kitchen. No one was there. I picked up the phone and called Sam, my old therapist. Even after two years I knew the number by heart. The phone rang twice and Sam answered.

"It's me," I said. "Ellen. I know it's been a while. But, Sam, I think I'm hallucinating."

"How interesting," he said.

"Someone's with you now?"

"How about calling back at eleven? You are all right, aren't you?"

"Fine, fine," I said. "Only hallucinating."

On the subway uptown I thought, it wasn't a hallucination at all. What I saw and heard couldn't be explained.

And then, amazingly, I forgot the whole thing. I went to the office, picked up the architects' manuscript, and spent the morning reading it. Eleven o'clock came and went, and when I remembered my morning call to Sam I felt foolish but obliged to call him back. Again a patient was with him, so I said I'd call at two. Channing and I ordered sandwiches and malts, and sat in the editor-in-chief's office eating and talking about the manuscript. By one, I was on my way to see the architects, planning what I'd make for dinner for Annie and me and thinking a little about Harry.

The architects were like their manuscript: disorganized, at

first quite charming, and then annoying. When we were through discussing the book, we had coffee and I found myself telling them what had happened that morning.

"A ghost," one of them said.

"That happened to me," said the other, and told me that one night his entire family, eight people, dreamed the same dream. He couldn't remember the dream, however.

Now it was three, and I realized I still hadn't spoken to Sam. When I called this time, he was free to talk, and I told him everything that had happened.

"It must have been frightening," he said.

"Yes." I was grateful. "Terribly."

"It sounds as if the place is haunted," Sam said.

"I think it must be. Or something. You don't think it's because I was angry at Harry or I'm in the city?"

"Why should it be?"

"Actually, it feels as if it has nothing to do with me at all," I said. "That's what makes it so peculiar."

I decided to make Annie a dinner of chicken, vegetables, and salad, and I beat my way through the rush-hour A&P to get the raw material. In the vegetable department, half the packages had been vandalized. The lettuce was limp. The deadline stamped on the chicken package was near. It was dark out and it began to rain as I left the A&P. By the time I made it to the liquor store, the paper bag of groceries was melting. The man in the store was nice and helped me repack the food. I bought a better bottle of wine than I would have otherwise, and continued to Annie's.

Again it took a few minutes to get the first door open. The light was out in the tunnel and I hurried into the courtyard. When I entered the apartment, everything was as it should have been. There was the hushed air of rooms empty for hours. I poured myself some of Annie's Scotch, put on some music, and started to make dinner. Annie has a lot of excellent and expensive cooking equipment, most of it covered by a thin layer of grease and dust.

When Annie came home, an hour and a half later, she called up from below and I hung over the bannister and watched her take off her coat and boots. "Exhausted," she said. "I am wiped out." Then she came upstairs and sniffed the air, saying, "Food. My God. Real food in my house." I started to say how easy it was to cook for yourself, when I remembered that when I lived in New York I ate home-cooked food only when someone else made it.

"Well," I said, "it's nice to be here."

Annie cleared her books and papers from the table, and began to set the table. I had just taken the chicken from the oven and was transferring it to a platter when the phone rang. We both stopped what we were doing. I remembered phones ringing in our college dorm and the suspense until it was announced who was wanted. Annie told me, half-relieved, half-envious, that it was for me.

"Look," Harry said on the phone. "Everything will be O.K. when we get a few things straightened out."

"Like what?" I said.

"Like the fact that you can't dictate what I'm going to do of an evening just because you're in town."

"Now, wait a minute," I said. "You said we were going to have dinner. I didn't imagine it, I didn't even suggest it."

"Ellen. Be real for once. I said we'd get together."

"In your letter you said we'd have dinner."

"Well. If you read that, you read wrong."

"What do you mean, 'if'?"

"I never wrote that."

"I don't lie," I said. "I don't lie. Who do you think you're talking to? One of your friends? I don't have any damn reason to lie where you're concerned." I would have gone on, but I saw Annie's face as she set the wineglasses on the table. She was trying not to hear, which was impossible. Worse, she was trying not to be upset. "I'm getting off this phone, Harry," I said. "There's nothing left to straighten out," and again I hung up on him.

Of course the minute I did and went back to the chicken, I

felt awful. While I recounted the conversation to Annie, I waited for the phone to ring, hoping he would try again, but he didn't. When we began eating, I gave up waiting.

"A strange thing happened this morning," I said to Annie, to change the subject. I told her then about seeing a woman in the apartment.

"What did she look like? What did she do," Annie interrupted.

"She was young," I said. "Blond. A strawberry blond, and she was wearing a duffel coat." I continued telling Annie about it—the way the woman had put her finger to her lips, her standing by the bed, her going upstairs.

"Patrick saw her too," Annie said. "But I thought . . . He's crazy, you know."

"What exactly did he see?" I asked.

"He saw her—the same hair, and she was young—but he saw her in a long white dress. She came into the bedroom where he was sleeping. I'd left for work already. When Patrick woke up and saw her, she did that too." Annie raised her finger to her lips.

"Then what?"

"She told him she was going upstairs. She said, 'I'm going upstairs now,' and then she went upstairs. But we explained all that."

"What do you mean you explained all that?"

"Well, he was very anxious. We'd just come back from my father's house. And what my shrink said was that it was really anger at me for abandoning him."

"What's that supposed to mean?"

"I left him and Cherie in the guest bedroom at my father's and I slept upstairs in my old bedroom without him. I left him in a strange house where he didn't know where anything was."

"And what did Patrick's shrink say?"

"He said Patrick was dreaming. That's all it was. A dream."

We ate the chicken and our talk drifted to our friends from college—where they were, who with, if anyone—and Annie's plans. "I've lived here for four years," Annie said, looking around the white room. "I've never lived anywhere so long. I went from school to school, from parent to parent, then with my husband, and then here. I painted it myself and figured out how to hang those plants on the pulley so they come down when I want to water them. I'm not going to apply to schools outside of New York. I'm not going to give up such a good apartment."

The phone did not ring again that night. Annie described a man she'd met recently and, listening to her discuss the prospects for a new relationship, I felt weary and envious. She is good at probabilities, and now that she's been through so much school, has a better vocabulary for disasters.

I slept well and in the morning woke at the same time Annie did. I started to pack right away. I was leaving New York that day after another session with Channing and the architects. I thanked Annie, and we discussed her coming up Easter or maybe in May. My friends from the city don't visit in the winter and I was leaving New York with the prospect of a long respite from their company. I felt relief edged with dread.

At the end of the day, I had to fight my way to Port Authority through the rush-hour crowds, dragging my suitcase and the manuscript, sweating underneath my winter coat and sweaters. I was dressed for my destination. The line for the night bus to Montreal was very long, and I could see the bus was going to be packed. I had my usual moment at the bus station. All during a visit I may think how odd city people are and how tenuous their relationship to the physical world. Then, on line for the journey north, I look at the other travelers, a little dumpier, slower, and more patient than I, and I am out of place once again. When the bus starts, I'm all right.

We came out of the tunnel into New Jersey, and I began thinking about the woman I'd seen, almost companionably, as one of the New Yorkers I was leaving behind me. She would stay there in the city with Channing and Annie, Harry and Patrick, and even with Dieter. I wondered for the first time since I'd seen her who the man was she expected and if he had ever joined her there. I wondered if it was their baby crying and what had become of their time together. I didn't think she was a dream. I know when I'm dreaming and when I'm not. I think now that she is a person who doesn't want to leave—that she, like myself and perhaps like everyone else, cannot bear for anything to end.

# The Smallest
# Loss

The first Saturday I was in London, I woke, finally woke, and felt that if I stayed in bed another minute I'd drown. Edward lay asleep and still. He used to talk in his sleep. Years ago, I heard him say, "You're fired." His eyes were closed and he was curled tight as a turtle, but he spoke distinctly. "I'm President," he said, then, annoyed, "You're Secretary of Defense. You're fired."

I went to the windows and pulled open the curtains but that didn't add much light. Edward had borrowed this apartment for us, just off the Finchley Road, one large room between garden and street. The garden had a small wooden gate that opened onto an unmowed field. There was a pony grazing in the field, even in the soaking rain.

I'd come to London full of things to tell Edward about our families and friends, about my time without him. But once I was with him it all seemed unimportant. Edward stirred in his sleep and raised one arm. He was lean and muscular, and I thought how I'd missed watching him make the simplest gesture. He opened his eyes, stretched, and saw me sitting beside the bed. "Been up long?" he asked.

"Not very long."

Edward turned to look out the window, and groaned. He reached out and pulled me back into bed. I lay against him still holding his hand. "It was three weeks straight sunshine before you came," he said. "I swear."

"I could leave. To improve the weather."

"No. I like having you right here. But we haven't done much, have we?"

"We must have done something." I'd been there six days. I touched his forehead where a frown was forming an arrow of a wrinkle.

"The British Museum has a show of prints. Japanese."

"A Dream of Fair Women," I said. "I've seen the posters in the Underground."

"Anyway, there's a nice restaurant in walking distance of the museum. We'll have lunch there afterward."

"You hate museums on weekends."

"Maybe London's changed me. You shouldn't hold me to everything I ever said."

We'd been together for so long—we'd met at college and married at twenty-two—that sometimes I had to look around to be sure he was with me, that I didn't simply assume that where I was so was Edward. Yet when we'd been married only three years, I had been ready to leave him. I packed my bags and lined them up at the door like little soldiers. Edward stood in our foyer, watching me. I was putting on my blue coat, looking at Edward in our hall mirror, when he asked me to stay. He couldn't tell me why I should. For once, he was at a loss for reasons. But it was enough for me that he wanted me to. How much more is it than that in the end, I asked myself then, and my answer has been our time together since.

When his firm offered a transfer to London, Edward agreed to go immediately. I had to stay in New York to finish up a phase of my research for an art foundation that was sponsoring a book on eighteenth-century American town plans. Edward had been hoping for some kind of change; he'd had interviews for jobs in San Francisco, Houston, and Boston. In London, he was doing the same kind of work for the same kind of clients, not precisely the point of moving, but he was tired of looking.

Once the rain let up on Saturday, we stopped in at a few
bookstores, then went on to the British Museum. As usual,
Edward's instincts were right; the central lobby was jammed
with people deciding where they wanted to go. We found our
way to the print exhibition upstairs, though I offered to skip
it.

"Fair's fair," Edward said, "and we've come all this way."

I paused by one small print, and when I looked up, Edward
was all the way across the room at the door. In the print a
woman dressed in a kimono was standing behind a bamboo
shade, looking out at a harbor. A ship was arriving. I could see
the harbor the woman was watching as well as the woman herself. Her hands were touching the shade.

"Better than I thought it would be," Edward said later,
though he seemed glad to be leaving. We were working our
way downstairs.

"How long since you've seen the Elgin Marbles?" I asked.

"Not long enough. Let's get out of here." Edward was heading for the main entrance.

I told him about the print of the bamboo woman and he
asked why I hadn't pointed it out to him. "You were all the
way across the room," I said. "I could tell you were ready to
go. But we can go back. I didn't know you cared about prints."

In the rain, we walked through the courtyard of the museum out to the street. A wrong turn on our way to the restaurant put us in front of an antique shop. In the window was a
small watercolor of a pink speckled fish. It was a lovely shade
of pink. We stood looking at it until Edward said, "Buy it if
you like it."

"I'm not sure how much I like it," I said.

He took me then to a restaurant on Charlotte Street where
the waitresses wore black dresses with white collars. On each
table was a white cloth and a pink flower. Another man would
go back another day, I thought, and buy the watercolor for
me, but not Edward. Yet if I wanted it, I knew I was welcome
to get it. Before he'd left for London, Edward had said that
plenty of couples were separated by circumstance and that it

would betray a basic flaw if our separation were to harm us. I'd worried that we'd made a mistake, but that afternoon I began to think it would be all right, that Edward and I could regain what we'd risked—taking each other for granted as you do the color of your own eyes or the weather.

We were to go to dinner at Penelope and Don's, friends from college whom we used to see when they visited Don's family in New York. By evening, the rain had stopped completely and we walked through St. John's Wood, then along Marylebone to Penelope's neighborhood. Edward had been to parties in two of the houses we passed; he described the rooms to me. His months alone in London had made him notice things I usually did and I was pleased. With only one look at his map, Edward led me along broad avenues and across the squares of Bloomsbury straight to Penelope's house. He was beginning to look English, I told him, but he said it was only his new raincoat. Though he's a large and solid man, Edward's pale coloring and high cheekbones made him seem fragile. We were always told how sweet we were together—Edward slightly worried and serious-looking, and I with the clear blue eyes, red cheeks, and unwrinkled brow of a girl on a package of cookies. Penelope, on the other hand, always looked glamorous. I said this to Edward as we turned into her street, but he didn't agree.

"She's just pretty," he said. "The way a lot of redheads are. She looks like my cousin Helen."

"She has so much energy. I feel as if I'm standing in a strong wind."

"You take her too seriously," Edward said.

Penelope lived in a Late Georgian square, three sides of which had been destroyed in the war and were replaced by modern public housing. Her side had survived in perfect shape. As we waited for her to answer the bell, Edward told me her flat occupied the garden and parlor floors.

"Have you seen her a lot?" I asked.

"Not all that often. Three months is a long time."

But when Penelope opened the door, it was as if two years, the time since I'd last seen her, was as no time at all. She might even have been wearing the same white shirt and silver-gray trousers—a combination that made her hair look brighter than ever and gave her green eyes an extra intensity.

"Corinne. Thank God! I never have enough women around," she said, and she gathered me in a hug. We were standing in a hall wide enough to accommodate several bicycles and skateboards, and floor-to-ceiling bookshelves. On the way to the kitchen, I glimpsed a large room filled with plants and paintings. The kitchen itself looked larger than it was because the floor was covered in white tile. A round marble table took up the center of the room. Enormous windows overlooked a cemetery, all that remained of a Victorian Gothic church. I could see a full-size angel in the twilight. The fragrance of honeysuckle came from a vine that was feeling its way through an open window toward a shelf of cookbooks.

"Where are the girls?" I asked. "Where's Don?"

"All in France," Penelope said. "Did Edward forget to tell you?"

I turned from the window. She was handing Edward a glass of Scotch, just light enough, just enough ice. That was how to be a femme fatale, I thought; have dinner with a man a few times and remember what he drinks. I asked, "What did Edward forget to tell me?"

"I'm getting divorced. I mean, I'm not legally because it's expensive and complicated. But we haven't been together for nearly a year. We're friends, of course, for the children. I had faith in our gossip network, Corinne, so I never wrote."

"Corinne lives in a world of her own," Edward said.

"It doesn't matter," Penelope said as she handed me a glass of iced wine. "Not anymore, after all this time. We went to France last summer. Actually, I joined Don there. He'd been attending a seminar outside Paris and I took the children there for our summer holiday. We met some people. This woman and her husband among them. Don fell in love with her and I don't blame him a bit. She's marvelous to look at. Very bright. I was friends with her first."

"That all sounds very civilized," I said, and thought it also sounded unlike Penelope; in college she kept men on a string and didn't tolerate rebellion, even from those she made fun of and didn't much care for. Unlike the rest of us, who learned to suffer our losses, Penelope hedged against even the smallest loss.

"You know me better than that." She laughed. "I'm not at all civilized. I was furious and I haven't spoken a word to her since they started sleeping with each other. But I was getting tired of being married. You know what marriage is, Corinne. You and Edward are practically the last married people of our old friends."

This wasn't true but I didn't want to argue. I felt sorry for Penelope, losing Don, whom I'd always liked. "I'm glad to be here," I said. "We'll have a chance to get to know each other again."

"We do know each other," Penelope said. "You always think people change. Anyway, we'll have to hold off until October."

"Why October?"

"Edward doesn't tell you anything, does he? I'm going to Japan for three months. I leave next week."

For dinner Penelope served pot roast at the round kitchen table, and I noticed how careful she was not to eat fat or potatoes. She hadn't changed much since college, only thickened in the way we all had. She looked more mature than I'd ever felt. It could have been having her children. Where I'd hovered above that decision for years, Penelope had plunged in early.

After dinner, we sat in the living room drinking brandy and coffee. Edward and I sat an arm's length apart on wooden rockers, opposite Penelope, who was stretched out on the couch. At one time, the room must have been both the front parlor and dining room, but someone had removed the double doors and made one huge space. Next to the

TV was a glass-fronted cabinet, filled with shards of marble and china, metal and stone figurines, seashells and feathers. Tables and chairs were draped with embroidered cloths Penelope had picked up in her trips around the world with Don. But it was Penelope's collection of plants that dominated the room. There was a rubber tree that must have been seven feet high, and next to Edward, leaning toward him, an Elephant Ears larger than any I'd seen outside of a nursery. Where the front window rose almost to the ceiling were built-in cabinets and on top of them more plants, some as tall as two and three feet. In this small jungle Penelope had installed wooden carvings of animals—a giraffe, an elephant.

"Where will you live?" Penelope asked. "Have you decided?"

"I've been looking," I said. "I don't know. I've seen a few places but nothing's right for us. Next step is a rental agency, I suppose."

"First day in London," Edward said, "Corinne was off, map in one hand, apartment list in the other."

"I've always hated it that you and Edward were in New York and I was here," Penelope said. "I won't have you move into some awful flat and be unhappy and return to New York. You must take your time and find the right place."

"Our time's almost up," Edward said. "The apartment we're in is only ours for another week." He reached for the brandy bottle. Edward hated theoretical discussions of practical matters. Either an apartment was there or not. And we'd decided that as long as I wasn't working, it was my task to find a place. I said, "We'll take what we can find for the moment."

"That's absurd," Penelope said. She sounded almost angry.

"Not really absurd," I said.

But she interrupted. "This flat is available for three months. Take it. It'll be my gift to you."

"We'll pay rent of course," I said. I looked at Edward, who didn't appear happy at this unexpected solution to our problem. "We'll talk it over," I said then, "and I'll call."

"What in the world is there to talk over? There's been a housing shortage in London since World War Two," Penelope said. "Take it. Just take it. I'll be offended if you don't."

We could always change our minds after we'd discussed it privately, so I said, "Done," and Penelope and I arranged that I would come the morning of her departure—in three days' time—to get the keys. Watering her plants was the only chore Penelope seemed concerned about. Edward didn't say anything. He went to Penelope's bookshelves and stood with his back to us, reading the titles.

When it was time to leave, Penelope watched from her door as we walked toward the taxi rank. The street was so quiet that when she closed the door, the sound echoed down the block.

"I'm not moving in there," Edward said quietly.

"What's the alternative? If we find something while we're there, we'll move out and I'll water the plants until she gets back. She's being very nice."

"I won't live there."

"It won't be for long. You can walk to work from there. And living in the neighborhood, I might be able to find something nearby."

"I hate Bloomsbury. I refuse to move into any place you find there."

"Did you have a fight with Don or something?"

"I haven't seen Don for years. I just feel awkward there."

"It won't be forever."


On Tuesday morning, I called Penelope. She was still sleeping, she said, though I thought I heard another voice in the background. She told me to be at the flat at one. When I arrived on time she looked more annoyed than glad to see me.

"Things are in an awful mess," she said. "I'll never get packed. People keep bothering me." As we passed the kitchen, I saw breakfast dishes for two and the morning papers strewn over the long table. Penelope's bedroom was downstairs. One wall was almost entirely windows; a set of doors opened onto a small patio. An Oriental screen showing a storm at sea stood next to a heavy carved vanity. A huge spider plant, a scented geranium, and all kinds of ivies hung in front of the windows. "Be careful of the Busy Lizzie when you close the blind," Penelope warned. "It gets caught sometimes."

There were two suitcases open on the bed and Penelope held up pieces of clothing for my advice on whether to take them with her. I was reminded of college, when one or the other of us was going away for the weekend. I almost always went to Edward's college, fifteen miles away, while Penelope actually attended legendary occasions like Winter Carnival. We toured the apartment and Penelope showed me the hot-water heater and the locks for the doors. She instructed me on watering and feeding the plants and told me to turn them every once in a while so they'd keep their shapes. She gave me Don's number in Paris and her extra set of keys and told me the name of a place where I could get a set made for Edward and where the best butcher and greengrocer and wineshop were in the neighborhood. The phone rang three times, and Penelope talked for a while with each caller, though she began by saying, "I can't talk. I'm out the door for Tokyo."

I began to think I was bothering Penelope by being there. It was always like that with her. Our meetings left me waiting for more, an intimate conversation, a quiet moment that never came. Penelope might have felt the same about me, for at the door as I was leaving, she said, "Why is it that we never really talk, Corinne? I wanted to hear everything about your life. You and Edward are my models for conduct."

"We're such models, there's nothing to tell but the day-to-day. Are you a gay divorcée or non-divorcée?"

"There's three men around," Penelope said, "but it's not all that gay. There are little misunderstandings, of course, but I feel really free, past the problems and the arguments." One of her suitors was older and very rich, she told me, also slightly famous. He was perhaps her favorite because he feared her more than she did him. He'd never married and assumed every woman wanted marriage from him, and how wrong he was, Penelope said, in her case. Another was very young—she smiled and then grinned—and very unstable, crazier than anyone she knew of any age. She'd just broken off for good from the third. He would never leave his wife, Penelope said, and I thought for a moment she would reach out and touch me. "I never wanted him to, Corinne. Honestly. But he didn't understand that ever, and that's why it had to end. Does all this sound awful to you? I think about you. Sometimes I wonder how you'd fare in my position."

"Differently," I said. "But we've always done things differently, haven't we? You probably think I've been married too long. Or maybe you don't."

"I just wonder what your secret is," she said. She smiled at me fondly and expectantly, as if I had wisdom I could dispense, if I chose.

I thought of a few things to say but decided against them, answering only, "If I told, then it wouldn't be a secret anymore."

Edward had a meeting outside London the next day, so I called for a taxi and moved our suitcases to Penelope's myself. There was still the smell of perfume in her bedroom. I tried to open a window but found they were all painted shut. Finally, I opened the doors that led to the patio.

I straightened the flat, putting away the clothing and books Penelope had flung about in her rush to leave. In college we went to antique stores, and I noticed among other goods she'd collected over the years some she'd bought then. She'd never learned to stop buying, nor had she  learned to part with what she had.

I shopped for food and drink, had a set of keys made for Edward, and then all I could think of was sleep. Edward didn't return until long after dark. He'd stood at the door, he said, ringing and ringing to try to wake me. When he came into the bedroom, he asked, "Couldn't we sleep somewhere else? I hate sleeping in other people's bedrooms."

"Not unless you want to sleep in the children's beds," I said.

"It's strange to be here."

"It's strange for me too," I said, meaning London, and then I fell back to sleep.

The cemetery was mostly lawn, with a few carved stones and a small grove of trees. In the mornings the cemetery was mysterious, like the beach before people get to it. It was a garden for children, really, and until eight, sometimes nine at night the children worked the cemetery in packs—hiding, running, resting in threes and fours on the grass. I could hear their conversations in snatches from the kitchen as I was cooking, or from the living room when I sat reading. I could never hear enough to make sense of it, but their shouts were clearly of rage or triumph, so different from the adult laughter and murmurings I heard from the neighboring houses at night.

Most afternoons I looked for apartments and continued to have no luck. I had one friend in London—Margaret, whom I'd met when she was in New York as a graduate student. She'd come to study the prints the foundation had in its collection. Margaret was married now and had a baby. I'd pick her up at her flat near Paddington and we'd put the baby in his stroller, and then we'd walk—to Church Street for vegetables and fruit, to Regent's Park to see the gardens. Margaret was a serene mother. When Tomtom did something particularly annoying, she looked at him carefully, giving him the benefit of the doubt, as if, perhaps, he had some idea there, better than hers. Watching them, I thought that finally it might be time for me to have a child. Soon it would be too late to have much choice. In London I had no job, nor did I plan to get one; and I could imagine having a baby in that city. I thought about the baby as I walked and window-shopped. I picked out a mohair blanket from a Scottish store, silver shoes from a shop in Covent Garden, a padded jacket from a Tibetan store. All my life, I'd been in school or at work. I'd never before been so free.

At Penelope's, every night before we went to sleep, Edward opened the doors to the patio and moved the screen to block neighborhood cats from entering. Aside from that, he might not have been living in Penelope's flat. He didn't like the pubs nearby and wouldn't go to any of them. He wouldn't help water the plants. He hated Penelope's knickknacks and said that he wanted to live in a series of empty rooms.

One night in August, Edward joined me for dinner with Margaret and her husband, and we left their house too late for the last Underground. We walked up Bayswater Road, hoping for a bus, but the ones that came were going in the wrong direction and there were no cabs. We walked for miles along Oxford Street, Edward pausing at the stores that sold hi-fis and appliances. I looked at the opaque cases, the padded speakers, the buttonless turntables, and took Edward's hand to make him keep walking.

"If I could buy anything," I said, "I'd get a mohair blanket for our bed . . ."

"Better find us a bed of our own first—"

"And that watercolor of the pink fish we saw. And some silver shoes."

"Get them," Edward said. "I didn't realize you were mooning around wanting things. Get them."

"No," I said. "I don't want them just like that, just to go from store to store and buy them."

"It's exactly like the way you eat ice cream. So carefully," Edward said. "Lick by lick. Saving it up."

That didn't seem particularly true, but by this time we were at the red-brick hotel near Penelope's street. I wished a pub was open or the hotel bar. I didn't want to go back to the flat, climb into bed, listen to Edward sleep and be caught by sleep myself. I wanted to keep going, though there was nowhere to go. I lagged behind Edward, who walked on at his steady pace.

He had his key in the door, waiting for me, when I caught up
with him.

In the near-darkness of the hall, the first thing I noticed was
the phone on the floor. The cord was slashed. "We've been
robbed or something," I said, but Edward was on his way to
the living room. In the dark, the room was quiet. The TV was
still there. We returned to the entry hall and when I turned on
the light, I saw red drops of blood shining on the carpet. Edward and I followed the trail of drops down the carpeted stairs
and onto the wood floors of the downstairs hallway into Penelope's room. Edward walked straight in. I stayed behind.

"Well, we know how he got in," Edward said.

The window was smashed. Pieces of glass were spread over
the skirt I'd left on the rocker. There was glass and blood on
my new straw bag. A Piggyback ivy had been thrown onto the
bed, and dirt had fallen from the broken pot. The Busy Lizzie
was stripped bare, its leaves scattered on the floor. I moved
toward the telephone by the bed and felt glass crush beneath
my feet. "I'm calling the police," I said.

When I'd given our address and reported the break-in to a
sergeant at headquarters, Edward and I went through the rest
of the flat. Downstairs, Penelope's was the only room touched.
In the upstairs bathroom, we found a carving knife in the
toilet, blade in the water. The knife was about two feet long.
I reached for it, but Edward held my hand before it touched
the knife and said, "Fingerprints. Maybe."

The water was discolored and I thought it was blood. "It's
only rust," said Edward.

I'd left the kitchen in perfect order. Now there was a saucepan on the sink and a small puddle on the floor with a sponge
lying beside it. "Blood and water," Edward said. "He tried to
clean up."

In the living room we found the worst of it, though I was
never sure if it was what he'd come for. The Elephant Ears lay
in pieces on the floor. The longest branch of the rubber tree had

been amputated and lay next to the trunk. Earth spilled from the broken pot. Everywhere I looked I saw broken pottery and slashed leaves and roots, mounds of earth. Pots had been hurled against the walls and onto the overturned chairs and the couch. The table lay on its side. All of Penelope's little arrangements—her ceramic animals, the bowl in the shape of a shoe—were turned upside down. I looked around for a place to sit, but there wasn't any. Edward was leaning against the doorjamb as if he were taking inventory.

"This is the biggest mess I've ever seen," I said.

Though we'd left the door wide open, the policemen rang the bell and waited politely for us on the stoop. There were two of them, the taller one a detective—Criminal Investigation Division, he told us. His name was Pettit. He was silver-haired and dressed in what I assumed was a disguise; blue jeans ripped at the left knee, a sweater that came halfway down his thighs. The constable, Williams, was rosy-cheeked and curious, and as we took them on a tour of the flat, he made appreciative comments. From their point of view I saw that the flat was of some interest. Starting with the bedroom, we showed them all we'd found, and when we reached the living room, Constable Williams commented, "Not a lover of plants by any means."

Edward and I stood silent. "Anything missing?" Pettit asked.

"It's hard to tell," Edward said. "At the best of times, you hardly know what's in the place—now you could hide an elephant. We're only guests here. As my wife explained."

"Personal," Pettit said. "In my experience, these incidents are usually personal."

"I find that hard to believe," Edward said. "With all respect to your experience, it's probably neighborhood kids."

"Stands to reason," Pettit continued in the tone of one whose mind is made up. "No sign of robbery. Nothing but silly mischief, though a bit sinister, I'll admit, this attacking of the plants. Only living things at home, you see. From the looks of it, you didn't come home a minute too soon—you must have just missed." Pettit turned to me. "Where were you tonight? Who knew you'd be gone?" He turned quickly to Edward, saying, "Not that it's any of my business, sir."

"We had dinner with friends near Paddington," I said.

Pettit surveyed the room, frowning at a small oil painting of a light switch. "And the lady whose flat this is, has she a husband?"

"In France with their daughters," I said. "They're separated."

"Pardon me for asking," said the detective, "but any boy-friends about?"

I waited for Edward to give me a clue but he was looking at the carpet and the broken pots. "I don't really know," I said. "We're friends from college, not current friends. I just came from New York." I wasn't going to tell him about the rich one or the crazy one or the married one. "I doubt this is personal. She isn't like this at all."

"Few people are," Pettit said, "until it happens. About the boyfriends . . ."

"Honestly. I don't know. I saw her for dinner. She offered us the flat."

"Nice of her to let you have it," Pettit said, "a nice-size place."

"That's what she's like," I said. What I was saying wasn't exactly true, but it seemed important to pretend it was. "Pe-nelope's a generous person. She gives and gives to all kinds of people. It could be a stranger. Someone who's watched her at the store."

"Possibly," Pettit said.

"It could have been anyone, Corinne," said Edward. "It doesn't do any good to speculate."

Pettit gave Edward a dark look, following, I supposed, the detective's rule of suspecting everyone. Edward was pale and haggard, ready for sleep. Pettit turned to me and appeared ready to start all over again about Penelope's boyfriends, hus-band, children, habits, possessions, so I said, "I have to go to sleep. This has been a shock and I don't have anything else to say."

Pettit hesitated, looking from me to Edward. Then he said, "The print men will be here in the morning. If there's anything you wish to add, either of you, please ring me. Nothing you care to add at the moment? Nothing you remember?"

Edward was out on the patio when I went into the bedroom. He was shaking off the blankets. He'd swept the floor near the bed and left a pile of glass and dirt in the corner. I watched him for a moment, waiting to be glad he was doing something.

"Let's lock the doors tonight," I said when he came inside. "There's plenty of air from the broken window."

Edward moved the screen in front of the open doors. "I can't sleep without air. Claustrophobia."

I began to undress. "How am I supposed to clean this?"

"I don't know. You'll do it the way you do everything. You'll start at some arbitrary point and get going. Then you won't look back."

"You make me sound very efficient," I said. "Or stupid."

"Look," Edward said. "I have to get up in the morning and go to work. We'll figure this out tomorrow night."

He got into bed and reached for me, to kiss me good night and position me so that he would be comfortable.

"I know who did it," I said.

"What do you mean?" He let go of me. "There's no way you could know."

"It was the young one," I said. "The one Penelope said was crazy. That's the only possibility I see. If she'd told me his name I'd get him over here to deal with his mess."

"What are you talking about?"

"There are three. That she told me about. There could be others. But the young one is the best candidate for plant-slasher. It couldn't be her favorite—the older rich one. This isn't his style. And the third one, the married man who thought she wanted him to leave his wife—he doesn't sound capable of this kind of effort." I turned on the light and got out of bed.

"I don't want to hear about this," Edward said.

"Why not? Were you so hurt when you caught on that she didn't want you to leave me? Or did you think you were breaking her heart?"

"Stop it," Edward said. "She shouldn't have told you."

"How stupid do you think I am?" I picked up the broken Busy Lizzie and shook some dirt on the floor. "This is your mess. I won't do it. I don't care. I don't care what you were up to with Penelope. I just won't clean this up. Not even for you."

I got back into bed and turned out the light.

"Corinne, I'm sorry," Edward said after a while. "It just happened and I didn't mean to get involved. I didn't know anything about the others."

"I'm sure you didn't."

"I wouldn't have left you. I had no such intention. She was the one who brought it up. That I would or wouldn't."

"I know you wouldn't," I said.

"I would never do anything to hurt you. I missed you terribly."

"No, you didn't," I said. "But it doesn't matter." I had the feeling that he was ready to tell me about the whole thing and I didn't want to listen. I put my hand on his mouth and he kissed my fingers. He held me against him in the way we fall asleep sometimes.

"It'll be fine again," he said after a while. "I see us years from now. In Venice."

"What are we doing in Venice?" I asked.

"We're laughing at this. At least smiling. Or maybe we're just drinking coffee. I missed you," he said. "I did."

The next day, Edward stayed home from work and together we put the living room in order. The print men came, and the glazier as well. Neither Edward nor I knew much about plants, but he remembered things from his childhood. I helped him prune limbs and leaves that were slashed beyond recovery and we tried to repot the plants that had been uprooted. For about a week the plants looked sad, then they got used to their new shapes. One of the print men said that the rubber tree might have been twenty years old, judging from its height. That was a far longer time than Penelope, Edward, and I had known each other, longer than I'd been married. The blood came up easily from the wooden floor with only warm water and a little soap. The carpet was shampooed, and once that was done, the stains that remained could have been made by anything at all —wine or tea, or even chocolate milk, spilled by a child on her way down the dark stairs to sleep.

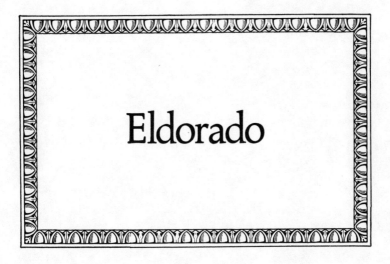

# Eldorado

The boy at the gas station was the first to notice the condition of the car. I go to that gas station because they check the oil and water whether I remember to ask them to or not, and this time the boy told me, "You're leaking oil all over the engine."

"The car's showing its age," I told him. "Put in more oil. Maybe it'll hold better this time."

That was in October. By December I had to face it. The car was taking oil every time I bought gasoline, and worse, if I tried going on the freeway—not just stop and start, but going somewhere—the engine missed. At forty-five, instead of rising into the next gear, it hesitated, then gave a burp. It could get to fifty but it didn't like it.

Christmas morning my daughter Melissa called and we had a nice talk about old times and a party she was going to that night. It was raining and dark, not the kind of day that makes you feel like doing anything. Still, it was Christmas, so I went to church, not because I'm so very religious, but it's what I'm used to doing. I keep things going in a certain way in my life. The condominium I bought when I sold the house is convenient in the way I like. I bought it when Melissa left home and I didn't need all that space to myself. Everything fits into it—the white couch and matching love seat, the flowered

drapes that remind me of a bush outside my bedroom window
back home. The drapes had to be hemmed and the furniture is
just that much too large for the room, but you notice that only
if you look closely and I'm not about to buy new furniture.

It's my first place on my own. In my parents' house I shared
a room with my sister, and when my husband was alive and
Melissa at home, you could call that sharing too. My daughter
seems young to be on her own, yet I was only a year older
when I married her father and took off, not just across the
breadth of Houston but all the way here from Maryland. I
don't regret that move for a minute. If I regretted it, I'd be
regretting my whole life, and then where would I be? Like so
many of the ladies I see in the store, I'd be wandering, wanting something but not sure what, and when asked if I could
use some help or suggestions, I could only answer that I don't
know, just looking.

I'm in ladies' sportswear at Battelstein's. On my store badge
I put my initials—T. C. Jefferson. I don't mind customers
calling me Mrs. Jefferson, but I don't want to be called by my
first name when all I've done is help match a skirt with a
blouse some odd shade of blue. It's part of my liking things to
look right, my being in the fashion business. When I first
went to work, when Donald was alive, it was a kind of hobby.
My friends call me Terry. My husband always used my full
name, Teresa. He said it made him feel like he was married to
a foreign woman. And I never called him Don or Donny or
Donny Joe. I called him Donald from the first time we met.

When the collection plate came around I gave five dollars,
five times what I usually give. I thought of when I was a little
girl and the minister at home talked about the homeless and
lonely, and sharing Christmas and our good fortune.

During the final hymn, I closed my eyes and tried to get a
picture of myself later that Christmas Day. I saw my kitchen,
and I was there, high heels kicked off, making myself a cup of
soup. That's all. And to complete the picture, there was the
Eldorado sitting outside my window, not shiny as it was when
Donald bought it, but still the car he always wanted. He could

have bought a Sedan de Ville but he said two doors were
enough for the two of us. Melissa was ten then and acting as if
she was already grown. He wanted it dark green, though it
was a custom color and held up delivery by six weeks. If he
could have seen the way dark green ages, he might have
changed his mind. I can't complain about the Eldorado. I
finished paying for it fourteen months after Donald died, and
it was still running seven years later.

The service ended and the congregation shuffled out, and
people were shaking the minister's hand. When it came to my
turn, the minister covered my one hand with both of his, just
the way the minister where we used to live did after Donald's
funeral, and I wondered if he could look at me and see me as
I saw myself, putting on that cup of soup, sore feet and all.

The Cadillac hesitated a few blocks from home, then the
engine stopped. When it rains, the streets in Houston get oil-
slick from the high shell content in the pavement, or so Donald always said. It's only because the Eldorado was such a
good heavy car that it didn't skid all over the place. The engine
started after a few minutes, and when I got home I parked the
car as I always did. I lost a hubcap a few years ago so I parked
with the side to the street that still showed two hubcaps.
That's the side where Melissa drove too close to a wall. I don't
know why she couldn't have stopped halfway, but she's always been like that. There was a deep scratch that ran from
one end of the car to the other. The passenger side was perfect
outside, though the carpet on that side was stained with something I could never get out. The air conditioning had been
broken for years, the radio only got two stations, and there
was all that oil leaking and the hesitating. Maybe it was a
screw loose and maybe it was the end of the world, but I was
ready to part with the Eldorado.

Inside the house, I kicked off my heels and made myself
that cup of soup. I settled at the kitchen counter where I could
look out the window and see the car and the woods next door
where the next block of condominiums will go. The billboard
across from me showed condominiums just like this bunch—

your choice of French, English, or Spanish style. Usually I keep the curtains closed, but I opened them to look at the car while I had my soup, waiting for some sign that I shouldn't sell it. I'd get a small car, I thought, an economy model, and then I'd take trips in it if I found someone to go with me. Maybe I'd go to New Orleans for Mardi Gras, something I've always talked about but never done.

The next day I composed an ad for the *Greensheet* and gave it to them over the phone. I knew Donald would say the exact right way to sell a car is to get the list price and deduct for damage, but I just guessed what the market would bear. I came up with an ad that said it all: *'68 Eldorado. 93,000 Miles. Runs. $500.00.* That seemed a little spare for ninety-three thousand miles of life experience with a car, but at twenty cents a word I wasn't going to tell the whole story.

I didn't get any calls right away. The paper came out Thursday and of course I work until nine that night. I was back home early enough Thursday and Friday nights for calls, but none came. I thought maybe I hadn't seemed enthusiastic enough about the car in my ad, maybe the bare truth is less than anyone will fork over five hundred dollars for. But Saturday morning as I was leaving for work, I got a call. It was a young girl, or sounded like one, and she had a list of questions: Was it a single-owner car? How were the tires? How was the body? I told her the bad news and the good, then she asked if I'd be home in the afternoon. I told her I'd be back by six but had to leave by seven. Melissa was meeting me for dinner at a new Japanese place out on Westheimer. That was at eight but it takes forever to get anywhere now, the city's so spread out. The girl said they'd be there on time and took my address.

They drove up in an old white convertible about the same age as the Eldorado. The girl was dark-haired and on the short side, but a pleasant-looking person. He was taller with lighter hair. They were dressed alike, denim jackets, denim pants. They walked around my car and she pointed to the scratch. He

crouched down to look underneath and she looked at the condominiums and the woods and the billboard. Then both of
them walked up the path to my door and rang the bell.

"Hello," I said. "I'm Mrs. Jefferson."

"T. C.," said the girl.

"I beg your pardon?"

"I see on your badge," she said. "Your initials, T. C. My
name's Jane and this is Jim."

"Come in," I said. "I just this minute got home from work.
Didn't even take off my badge." Donald always warned me
about letting strangers in the house, but I said, "Come in." I
motioned for them to take a seat and they settled side by side
on the white couch. I took the love seat opposite and said,
"Well, if you have any questions. You can see there's some
things wrong and I can warn you—it's leaking oil. All over.
And the air conditioning doesn't work either." Jim made a
gesture with his hand as if to say, "Air conditioning, what does
that matter?" and I continued, "You can see the scratch down
the side. What a shame. That car was a gift from my husband,
who's dead now, a gift to both of us, really. He loved that car.
The most comfortable car in America, Donald used to say."

"How long has it been leaking oil," Jim asked.

"A few months," I answered. I could see he didn't care if
Donald was alive or dead, not in an unfriendly way, just busi-
nesslike. But I saw a flicker in Jane's eyes and she looked
around the room as if I'd handed her a key to me.

"And you don't know why it's leaking oil," he said.

"No. I'm thinking of buying a new car, a smaller car. Just
me alone, I don't need such a big car. Would you care to drive
it?"

"Actually," he said, "we're waiting for our friend Bobby.
We just got to Houston, you see, and I don't know anything
about cars really. He's worked on Cadillacs."

I looked at my watch. "Well, I'll have to be going in half an
hour. I'm meeting my daughter at a new Japanese place. Way
out on Westheimer, and you can't tell about traffic." I offered
them coffee, but they both declined it. To put them at ease, I

asked them about themselves. "What will you do in Houston? Do you have jobs?"

"I just finished engineering school," Jim said, "and Jane's not sure what she's doing."

"That's a coincidence," I said, "because Donald was a structural engineer. That's why we came to Houston ourselves. Even years ago it was the place to come. You'll make your way here if you work hard. So many people come here. A thousand a week, the paper says, and I guess that includes children."

Jane smiled. "It's just us," she said. "We don't have any children."

"Whereabouts are you looking to live? If you're thinking of a condominium, you might as well have a look at this one. They're going up all over town." From the looks of them and from their interest in my Eldorado, I didn't suppose they had much cash, but it never hurts to be helpful.

"Sure," Jane said. "I always like looking at other people's houses."

I showed them downstairs first, not that there's much more than you can see from the couch. There's the small bedroom I always keep ready in case Melissa spends a night at home. They seemed to like it, and Jim said it was a nice big window for a room that size. The window lets in too much light, so I keep the curtain closed to protect the carpet and bedspread. Donald was particular about protecting furniture.

Upstairs, the first thing you see is my bed and I don't know what triggered me off, but I said, "It's my first place. I got this place for myself really. Though I keep that downstairs room for Melissa." I saw them looking at the king-size bed and the drapery I have over the cushioned bedboard. "It's the first time I've been alone," I said. "I love it. I don't think I'll ever remarry. I meet men but none of them are worth it. They want more than I have to give. I had my marriage. I respect Melissa for leaving home. I wasn't much older than she is when I left home and came all the way to the bottom of Texas with Donald. It's only healthy she's gone, young as she is."

I showed them the balcony outside the bedroom. "It's not big," I said, "but it's pleasant to sit here if it's not too hot, and this high wall protects you from the neighbors. I could sunbathe nude if I were that kind of person."

"I used to like Sunday mornings," Jane said. "When I lived alone. It's all a question of how you like yourself, isn't it, whether you can be alone."

"It sounds right," I said, "just like living with another person you like."

"It's a good-size condominium," Jim said. "Maybe sometime we'll be able to afford one."

I took them downstairs again, but since their friend still hadn't arrived, Jane asked if they could come back in the morning. "Bobby's jogging," she said, "and he probably lost track of the time." I told them I'd be back from church by noon and they'd be welcome to bring him then.

"I like the looks of the Eldorado," Jim said. "Don't sell it to anyone but us," and he smiled for the first time.

There was a traffic jam where Westheimer meets Hillcroft, don't ask me why. I try not to get tense and angry in traffic jams the way Donald used to, so I thought about Jim and Jane doing the same thing Donald and I did years ago. There was nothing wrong with our life, nothing I can say I wish had gone one way when it went another, short of Donald dying when he did. I thought of things to say to both of them— "Don't waste your money on furniture right away," "Don't expect too much when he comes home from work. It takes it out of a man to work every day, day in, day out." I never said these things to Melissa either, and by the time traffic started moving again I was feeling sad about all the things I had to say that I probably wouldn't ever say to anyone, and if I did they would sound dumb anyway.

I say to customers in the store, "If you're not born beautiful, you have to make yourself beautiful," and most of the time they just smile and ask me if I think it looks all right, the blouse or skirt or ensemble, but some of them look startled and I realize I've said the wrong thing. They hoped they were beautiful, you see, and doubted it at the same time. So my saying that hit them just the wrong way, and I knew Jane and Jim and Melissa would think I was speaking to the wrong people, that their lives would never be like mine. The customers still buy, most of them, but that's not the point.

I got to the restaurant before Melissa and chose a table where I could see the door. It must have been a Hawaiian restaurant before it became Japanese, because it had that kind of dark carving you see at Trader Vic's over at the Shamrock. At both places they serve drinks you just know will come in plastic pineapples or coconuts. Donald and I went to Trader Vic's once and didn't think much of it.

When I'd waited twenty minutes for Melissa, I went ahead and ordered a Scotch. When Melissa didn't come after an hour and the Scotch was long gone, I could tell the waitress wanted the table. There was a line of couples out on Saturday-night dates waiting to eat, and there I was, alone, with my empty glass. I'd come all that way, I thought. I could have ordered some oysters tempura on my own, but I'd lost my appetite. I drove home and made some soup, watched the news on TV, and fell asleep. I could have watched the late movie, but it was a horror film and they always give me nightmares.

Melissa called just after eight the next morning. I knew she was really sorry, otherwise why would she be up so early on a Sunday morning? At the last minute she'd been asked out on a date and she'd tried to call me to cancel, but first my phone was busy and then there wasn't any answer. I hadn't been on the phone all afternoon—I'd been at work—but I didn't want to start an argument with her. I did remind her she could have called the restaurant, but she said they were in a movie that started at seven-thirty. We made another date for Monday night. For Melissa to come to my house for dinner. I was looking forward to seeing Jane and Jim again. I'd thought of some real-estate people they could see about a place to live, though Jim's last remark about money made me think they couldn't afford to buy right away.

Sunday was dark and sultry, just on the edge of rain. When I got back from church there was an old red Volkswagen parked in front of my place and a young man was sitting in it. He watched me as I parked and walked up to my door, then he called out my name. He came up to me and said he was Bobby, Jim and Jane's friend, come to check out the car. I handed him the keys and told him he was welcome to drive it. "I'm starved after church," I said, "so you're on your own. That's why people go to church, you know, to work up an appetite for Sunday lunch." Bobby smiled and took the keys from me. I went inside and as I was changing from my church suit I remembered Donald always reciting that old saw about church and Sunday lunch. There were times when I knew he was going to say it, and then he did, and I thought I would lose my mind anticipating a lifetime of Sundays and that joke. But that was just part of thinking he'd be around forever. You don't marry a man expecting him to keel over from a heart attack at the age of forty-two. When Donald died I couldn't sleep for crying. The pills the doctor gave me put me out only for an hour or two. I'd wake in the morning before the light and feel so desperate. The only thing that calmed me down was to go out to the Eldorado and sit there, just as I was, in my nightgown. I didn't care who saw me sitting there behind the wheel, it was such a comfort to me. No one saw me. No one else was up at that hour. I did that for five mornings, then I felt strong enough to stop.

I decided on chicken pot pie for lunch. The oven was pre-heating when Bobby shut the hood, got into the car, and drove away. I waited for some feeling of regret at seeing the car go, even for a test run, but there was none. I opened the Sunday paper to the car ads, and was balancing my life between a Ford Granada and a Dodge Aspen when the Eldorado pulled up again. Bobby parked it with the wrong side showing, then came to the door. I wondered where Jim and Jane were. They'd have the energy to fix the car, and milk a few more years out of it, just running from one end of town to the other. The pie was almost ready when I let Bobby in. He accepted my offer of coffee and sat at the kitchen counter.

"It really needs work," he said. "I don't know that much about cars, but I wouldn't be surprised if it needs a valve job."

"Still, it's cheap at the price," I said. "They'll get good value if they treat it right. I know I haven't, but it isn't too late." So he wouldn't think I was giving a hard sell, I said, "By the way, before I forget, I have the names of some real-estate dealers for Jane and Jim. Are they coming soon?" Bobby looked puzzled, so I explained, "They were interested in a condominium like this one."

"I don't know about that," Bobby said. "I thought they were looking for a car that doesn't need work to get them to L.A. next week. I mean, your Eldorado has a lot of potential, but it needs a lot of work. A Cadillac's never really cheap. Parts alone."

"But they looked at this condominium," I said. "They told me it was just the one they'd want." Bobby didn't argue with me. He seemed like a nice quiet person who says what he has to say and that's the end of it. "I must have misunderstood," I said. "I guess the car is fated to live and die in Houston, just like me."

When Bobby left, I took the chicken pot pie from the oven. It had passed the point of hot and gone on to dry. I wondered why Jim and Jane had lied to me about moving to Houston and settling here. Maybe they'd lied about everything—even about being married, and him being an engineer. Why did I show them my place and tell them about Donald and me? I went to the window and looked at the Eldorado. There it sat, big and useless. If it hadn't been a Sunday, I'd have driven it to the nearest used-car lot and gotten rid of it there and then.

I telephoned Melissa, just to talk to someone who knew me, but she wasn't home—why should she have been on a Sunday afternoon? The rain that had threatened all morning started down, and since the windshield wipers on the Eldorado didn't always work, I couldn't go anywhere even if I'd had somewhere to go. I went upstairs and lay down in bed, and I tried to take comfort from the clean sheet, from knowing the blanket was the right shade of blue for my eyes. Just when it seemed I would have to get up and figure out something to do with myself, I fell asleep. I slept away the afternoon in a deep kind of trance, and woke at six with a different feeling. I didn't feel ashamed of myself, nor did I feel I'd been tricked, for I figured the thing out in my sleep. Jim and Jane hadn't really lied to me, any more than I lied to Melissa when I said to her, "You go. Cut the apron strings. I'm fine by myself." It's a luxury we have, to tell people what we'd like to be the truth of our lives, and it's the feeling behind the lies that makes them acceptable to both parties.

The next evening when Melissa was over for supper, the phone rang. A man came along an hour later and bought the Eldorado in fifteen minutes. I told him the truth about the car, but he waved it all aside. He wanted a car for his son to fix up, he said, so his boy could learn the value of making things work.

# The
# Glass
# House

*A Novella*

Longtemps je t'ai construite, ô maison!
A chaque souvenir je transportais des pierres
Du rivage au sommet de tes murs
Et je voyais, chaume couvé par les saisons,
Ton toit, changeant comme la mer,
Danser sur le fond des nuages . . .

House, I took a long time to build you!
With each memory, I carried stones
From the shore to the top of your walls
And I saw, thatch mothered by the seasons,
Your roof, changeable as the sea,
Dancing against the clouds . . .

From Louis Guillaume, "Maison de Vent,"
in *Noir comme la mer*

Arla couldn't have driven faster if wolves had been nipping at her snow tires, or if it had been a night in June instead of what it was—March. The road was clear all the way home, and in less time than usual she reached the car wash that sat at the edge of town. Its big sign—Robo—was stuck on a pole ten feet in the air. The sign was white, plastic, and shining in the icy night, and the building—red aluminum siding nailed to a wooden frame—was parting gradually from its structure. The town was dark, though a few lights shone through lace curtains. Climbing the hill at the Catholic cemetery, the back wheels swerved on an icy patch, but after that the ride was smooth. The last half-mile was downhill until she reached her dead-end road. At the first of a row of maples, the road rose, then dipped into a small valley past her neighbors', then rose again to the barn, where Arla left the car. She made her way across the yard to the dark house and wished, as she'd wished before, that she had the mercy to leave a light on for herself. She opened the door and stood in the dark, listening to the furnace click on and the refrigerator hum, and Arla knew she'd missed another day in the house by being in the museum.

The back room was heated only by the wood stove, and the fire was down to embers. She might have let it go out the days she worked, but Arla needed the warmth when she walked in, and the reassurance that the house stayed alive each day without her. Now, as she renewed the dying fire, Arla thought of the museum fifteen miles away, its white columns harshly lit by outdoor spotlights. She saw fire starting somewhere—the storage space, her office—and saw it traveling through the museum, consuming the walls and melting the windows, melting the glass that covered the paintings, in the end exploding in the wooden building. Sometimes she had this vision when she was at the museum; then the fire was in her house and started with the wood stove. Arla shut off the light in the back room and entered the main part of the house.

The house Arla lived in had been her mother's, bought after she divorced Arla's father. Her mother hardly missed a weekend there in the ten years between the divorce and her death. At first, she liked the house as it was—"beat-up," she said— but as time went on and especially as she began to feel ill, she wanted the house to be as pretty as it could be. She remodeled her bedroom and part of the kitchen before she was too weak to leave the hospital. Arla remembered the last weekend in the house with her mother and an old friend of her mother's. Arla was on vacation from boarding school, and her mother wanted them to have Thanksgiving together in the country house.

Going over the memory, Arla could not decide if the holiday had been more trouble than it was worth, for everything had been trouble: packing and driving to the country from New York—because her mother could walk sometimes, and sometimes a step exhausted her; being there—for the friend and Arla cooked and cleaned while her mother directed from a rocking chair they'd brought into the kitchen for her. Her mother had wanted the table set in a certain way, napkins and cloth, crystal and silver brought from the city, as if the table looking right would make everything else all right. She couldn't digest the food, or almost none. When Arla went to the bathroom in the middle of the night, she found her mother in the rocker in the dark kitchen, crying. Arla said nothing about the tears, but offered to sit with her mother. She was only sixteen years old, she told herself now, and could not have known what to say to a woman sitting in the dark crying perhaps because she was dying, perhaps for her divorce or because her child was growing up. It could have been for some reason Arla wouldn't hit on in a million years of guessing. Her mother had told her, No, she should get her sleep.

For the rest of the weekend they played Monopoly. They left on Saturday afternoon, a day early, when her mother admitted she needed to be back in the hospital. She hadn't said she was glad they had Thanksgiving together in the house, but Arla assumed she was glad. Arla thought about those days for years, thought of ways in which she could have been more cooperative and sensitive. In truth, she'd wanted to close herself off from the dying woman and only hoped it hadn't shown.

When her mother died, the house was sold to pay for the rest of Arla's education. Her father had remarried a year after the divorce, and when her mother became ill, Arla was sent to a boarding school in Connecticut. In order to save money the first year she was at school, Arla lived not in the dormitory but with the family of the math teacher. It was a nice house, one her mother admired, but it was a few miles beyond a walk or even a bike ride when the weather permitted. The math teacher took Arla to school and drove her home every night. Even later, when Arla lived in the dormitory and did everything all the other students did, she didn't feel as if she'd really arrived yet at school. She always felt she was still in the math teacher's car, looking back at the other students as she was driven away from campus for the night. On holidays, she went to New York and stayed in her father and stepmother's guest room. Her mother was never mentioned, and over the years Arla came to see that her father was an oblique man who lived with his lives cut and placed separately, like the pieces in a cubist portrait.

Arla found her mother's house again by accident. After college, she moved to New York City and began working as a receptionist in an art gallery on Seventy-ninth Street off Madison Avenue. Arla was invited to spend New Year's weekend upstate with a group of friends from college. The country was familiar. She hadn't asked before they left the city exactly which town they were heading for, and the name hit her as any memory of her mother, with pain. The second day they were in the country, she went for a ride with a friend who wanted to look for antiques, and Arla found the house. She had seen bits and pieces of it in dreams and memories for years, and Arla recognized it immediately. She asked her friend to stop, and they sat in the car looking at the house until Arla said they should go on to the antique store.

There was no one to talk to about the house. Her father had never seen it. Her mother's friend had moved to California and had stopped sending Christmas cards years before. Arla returned on her own in the spring and talked to a local real-estate agent. If the house ever came on the market, she told him, let her know first. From then on Arla waited for the house, as if her future were set and she had only to catch up with it. Her job at the gallery ended and she found a job at an art publisher's, where she learned to put together exhibition catalogs for large museums. She looked at the other editors and at the rows of books and catalogs in the firm's library. She wondered if in ten years she would be able to point out the volumes she'd worked on as the others could, but that wondering was a game. The real thing was the house.

In the two years it took for the house to come on the market, Arla had affairs: with a reporter for ABC News who had been wounded in Vietnam; with a medical student, the brother of an editor. She went to Montauk for a weekend with him. They stayed in a rickety hotel off the highway and took pictures of each other on the beach. His skin was smooth and thick, and he was strong as she never felt herself to be. He showed her his right forearm, far larger than the left, an achievement from the summer when he was sixteen and scooped ice-cream cones at the World's Fair in Queens. There was a sunniness about him she craved like a sweet, and Arla kept photographs of them smiling on the beach long after she stopped seeing him. She looked for a sequence, a recognizable progression of feelings, but the affair began and ended out of her control and beyond her understanding. It wasn't too hard when it ended. She had been waiting since her parents were divorced for something to happen, and the something was neither being sent to school nor her mother's death nor a lover nor a job. This was what it was, the house.

The house might never have come on the market. But Arla wasn't surprised when the real-estate agent called her. Her mother's name appeared on the deed, two owners past, but the lawyer who handled the sale didn't notice or didn't care. Her father commented on the coincidence of her buying a house in that town, but Arla didn't take up his hint and tell him it was her mother's house. She borrowed half the down payment from him; the rest she secured from the sale of a painting she'd bought little by little when she'd worked at the art gallery. Around the time she was getting ready to leave the city, Arla was working on a catalog for a show Monique Martin was putting on at a cousin's museum in northern California. When she told Monique she would be leaving the publishing house and moving to the country, Monique invited her for tea in her town house on Sixty-second Street. They sat in the drawing room on opposing black satin couches. The floors were polished parquet. On the walls hung small paintings by minor and major surrealists and a pastel of a parquet floor. The marble fireplace was laid with silver-birch logs the color of the walls. A maid served tea; Monique and Arla discussed the museum Monique was founding near Arla's house. Monique had a bad cold and sat upright, her long legs at a becoming angle to her body. She was tall and ash blond, neither pretty nor not pretty; a definite sort of face. Arla saw that, years before, Monique had made up her mind that certain colors and materials would do for her, others would not, and hadn't reconsidered since. She wore violet and gray, black and white. Arla thought they would get on. Monique was older by ten years or so, and this seemed an advantage. The only obvious misunderstanding was that Monique expected Arla to live in a small house she owned in the area and to take the house as part of a much-reduced salary.

Arla wasn't surprised at finding the job, though that too could have taken a lifetime. She was twenty-seven when she moved to the country. She told one friend that the house she'd bought was her mother's house, and the friend didn't think it was peculiar. Her father and stepmother thought she was taking on a lot, but encouraged her to do it if she wanted to. The two families that had owned the house between her mother and Arla had changed the house sufficiently so that the only sign left of her mother's sojourn was the bookshelves in the bedroom.

As she changed into her nightgown and washed for sleep, she listened to the TV news. She brushed her teeth to the college hockey scores, waited through the dull jokes between newscasters and the commercials, and then came the weather. Fifty-percent probability of snow by morning, changing to thirty by afternoon.

Arla lay in bed waiting for sleep. In nine hours she would be at the museum again. She had worked that day from eight in the morning until ten at night, getting things ready for Monique and Leon, Monique's father. They rarely visited together, even more rarely in winter; one or the other arrived for the big shows of spring, summer, and fall. They traveled separately, Monique insisting on saving time by flying and Leon preferring the safety of the train. Arla had ordered flowers for the museum, a touch Leon Martin liked and Monique hated. She said cut flowers made her think of funerals and nothing else.

In nine hours Arla would be at the museum again, and now she couldn't sleep thinking of the road, of getting there. She thought of her desk: folders were piled neatly, waiting for Monique and the decisions she would make, decisions that took a word from Monique and inches of paper for Arla to carry out. They spoke on the telephone weekly, sometimes daily, but there was always a pile-up of decisions on possible shows, loans, traveling shows, the condition of the building and the collection, future long-term projects. Every few months Arla went to New York to see Monique; this time Monique was saving Arla the trip. Her heart speeded up when she saw car lights outside her window; then the lights swung away, only reflections in the glass. It was a neighbor, one of the Clifford boys, returning from the ski mountain where he worked. With the slam of his door, Arla relaxed and after a while was asleep.

Up before dawn on Tuesday, not much of a trick in winter, but Arla enjoyed beating the light even by five minutes. She stood, cold, her nightgown billowing from the hot-air register beneath her feet, and she watched the sky lighten over the hills. New snow had fallen in the night. A cow's breath could be seen across the field, the red cow covered with snow. Arla went into the back room and renewed the fire in the wood stove, then got ready for work. She chose a blue silk shirt and black wool trousers, knowing that the intense blue showed off her eyes and the pallor of her skin. Monique liked that shirt— she'd once told Arla that with her dark hair and blue eyes, she should always wear cold colors. Arla bent forward and brushed her hair forty times, then flattened it by pulling her black cashmere sweater over it. The sweater was a graduation present from her father, brought back from London, where he'd gone with Arla's stepmother. Arla looked in the mirror and took the extra time to put one kind of cream around her eyes, another on her face. The climate was drying her up, but she wasn't looking leathery yet, the way some country women did. There was an expression most women took on when they looked at themselves in the mirror. Though Arla disliked its blankness and intensity, she recognized it in her-self. Rouge, lipstick—she was ready for work.

At the kitchen window, Arla waited for the water to boil and watched her neighbor ride past on his tractor, gone to his father's farm on the next road for hay. She wondered why Monique and Leon were coming to the museum. She wondered if their visit meant that something had gone wrong. Though there were reasons for the museum to exist—Monique owned the building and the land, Monique wanted a place for her collection, needed a tax write-off—it had always seemed to Arla that for all her careful work, the museum could disappear or be destroyed at any time. Arla's work was the rock on which the museum rested, or at least the credibility of the museum. She had no training and no experience in museum work, but Arla had created the museum's systems: for cataloging the collection, for making exhibition catalogs of different types, for press releases and invitations to shows. Her title was "museum registrar"; she did the work of a registrar and more. Each object was assigned an acquisition number: on loan, traveling to Europe and across the United States, the object was followed by Arla and her systems. In four years, none had been lost, none set aside in the basement of a great museum or the warehouse of a shipper never to be seen again, and none had been broken. Each object had a title, each artist's name was spelled consistently in every piece of museum literature and correspondence. Each object was measured, and its dimensions, medium, date, provenance, and condition were noted on its own card in the master collection file. The file system was impeccable; all objects, artists, shows, and inquiries about shows were filed and cross-filed. Everything was accessible.

It had taken Arla four years to accomplish this task and to undo Monique's system of letters in cardboard boxes and shopping bags and of cards filed by medium, a system that Arla found almost hostile in its uselessness. Things were quieter now in the museum. There were fewer crises, fewer times when Monique woke Arla at midnight to say she was sure a painting was lost or on loan when it was not. Monique's voice was the same, day and night—impersonal, demanding, humorless. Arla poured the boiling water into the coffeepot and thought of her house and how she could survive without the museum. It was the best job she could get, and she did her best at it. At the beginning, she'd felt lucky to have the job.

Now that she'd had so much experience at it, had handled so many problems, worked so hard, Arla felt there should be more reward than watching the smoother daily functioning of Monique's museum. But even if she found a better job, she would never find one so close to her house.

The museum sat on a wedge-shaped piece of land elevated from the highway, so that the building and grounds could be seen at once. The main part of the museum was perfectly square, a heavy centered portico emphasizing the symmetry of windows and chimneys. Wings had been added at a later date, placed carefully in the same strict symmetry as the main building: in one wing were Arla's office and the storage space; in another, one room had been made of two to exhibit larger modern paintings. The building was clumsy, Arla knew, the columns too heavy, the symmetry too rigid, but it always looked completely honest to her, standing up so straight on its hill. Monique had inherited the house from an American aunt, her mother's sister, and had supervised its conversion from a large Greek Revival farmhouse to a functional museum. When the property first came into her hands, she'd intended to sell it. One thing led to another, and it became the museum. From her own and her family's collection, Monique brought prints, tapestries, ceramics, glass, silver, pewter, wooden carved figures, paintings, toys, posters. There were a few minor works by major artists and a series of four paintings by a New York color-field painter commissioned by Monique for the East Wing; but the museum was by and large a place for work whose uniting characteristic was that it appealed to Monique or her father, Leon.

Once the museum was remodeled and the collection installed, Monique's decision made sense. The museum was near the borders of Vermont, Massachusetts, and New York, an area that boasted several colleges, leaf tourists in the fall, ski tourists in the winter, and many summer residents. It lay within an hour of Albany and the more established Clark Art Institute in Williamstown. The logic of the location, so evident in retrospect, pleased Monique. Her act of will was now spoken of as natural and inevitable, and she didn't like to hear it mentioned that she'd ever thought of selling the place or doing anything with the property but creating her little museum. Monique was the person least given to reminiscence of anyone Arla knew. She was also unwilling to hear of anything negative, and Arla had learned to call problems and snags and difficulties "details," sometimes "details that required Monique's attention." Arla could declare matters to be important, but never "urgent," certainly never "emergencies."

To complete the museum, Leon had sent his master gardener up from Connecticut. The gardener's presence on the place had been like a long shadow on a summer lawn; in his silence and persistence, he reminded Arla of her mother. Even now, in March, even through the snow, she could see his work. More than the actual renovation, the landscaping had transformed the house into a formal building.

When she arrived, Arla saw that Bob Walters had opened up the museum. He worked as handyman, guard, at times as assistant registrar. He and Arla were the only full-time paid workers at the museum; a cleaner twice a week and various volunteers completed the staff. Arla walked through the central lobby to the empty storage space. One show had just been crated up and shipped off, the next was due to arrive in two weeks. Bob stood at the electric coffee machine, watching the red light and listening to the coffee perk. He didn't move when Arla walked up beside him. He was a large, bearded man, taller than she remembered him day to day. They both looked on Monique more as a force than a person, but nothing Monique did or didn't do mattered to Bob so long as she kept the museum going. Bob lived nearer to the museum than Arla, in the woods at the end of an old logging road, in an odd-shaped house he and his wife had built when they moved upstate six years before. When he'd finished his house, he was out of money. At that point Arla, Monique, and the museum appeared in his life. When she thought of Bob, Arla thought only that people were different from one another, for Bob expected things to work out more or less—and more or less, they did. Arla hung her jacket in the closet with Bob's tools and checked the thermostat. It was set at sixty-five, and the museum always felt cold. Americans needed too much heat, Monique said.

"I'm worried about the snow," Arla said.

"Don't worry about the snow," Bob said. "It'll take care of itself."

Arla reached for the phone and dialed the Albany airport. Bob set a cup of coffee on her desk, and when she'd finished talking to the airline Monique was flying, she told Bob, "No planes. Maybe all day."

"No Monique," he said.

"Well. That's terrific." Arla looked at her watch. Leon's train was due to arrive in an hour and a half. "I should be leaving now to pick up Monique. It's just like her not to tell us she can't make it."

"I'm glad I'm just the hired help," Bob said. "I'm going up front. In case someone wants to come in early out of the snow."

There was no answer at Monique's town house, and Arla imagined the phone ringing in the black satin drawing room. The noise of the snowplow coming up the circular driveway reached Arla's office. She followed the noise around the back to the parking lot and down the driveway. Her office was nothing more than a corner of the storage space, partitioned by Masonite. The partition ended eight feet up, and the space from there to the ceiling was fenced in with heavy wire mesh. Arla had asked Monique for a better office, but Monique hadn't responded and Arla had grown used to the place as it was. It seemed like a lot of trouble now to contemplate moving her files and stacks of catalogs, the books and art magazines, even the calendar on the wall. She accepted the office as part of the job.

Arla hung up after twenty rings. She was thinking of paging Monique at Kennedy when the museum phone rang.

"Arla? Is that you? This connection is so dreadful."

"I can hear you perfectly," Arla said.

"Perhaps I should ring you back. No. You call me, that's much simpler. Here is the number. It is a phone booth. If you could see this airport," and Monique hung up.

When they'd reconnected, Arla asked, "Better?"

"The people in back of me are breathing fire. We must be brief," as if Arla were detaining her.

"I called the airline. I guess you won't be making it today."

"It really is a nuisance. But I have to be back in New York by five-thirty, so it is impossible. You'll handle everything, I'm sure, and we'll talk tomorrow. Tell my father I regret missing him," then Monique disconnected.

Midmorning, Arla stood at the entrance door, waiting for Leon to arrive. The driveway was covered again with a light layer of snow, but the snow was dry and powdery and didn't threaten traction at the moment. When the volunteer's car pulled up, Bob Walters went out to help Leon across the snow and up the museum steps. Leon got out of the Volkswagen with a little difficulty. Another man got out of the backseat; then the volunteer waved and drove off. Despite the falling snow, Leon and the stranger remained outside, looking up at the museum.

"Ah, Arla," Leon said when he entered the museum. "You see how devoted I am to the museum to come today. Here is my young colleague, if he will permit me. Joseph Bird. Architect."

"Architect," Arla said. She held out her hand to Joseph Bird. He was a large man and young. His hair was darkened by the melting snow but it looked as though it would go blond or red if there were any sun. He wore gold-rimmed glasses that accentuated this potential blondness, and his face, while handsome, didn't strike Arla as the important thing about him. His size was important, and his solidity. Leon looked smaller than ever next to Joseph Bird, older than his seventy years, more fragile than Arla remembered him. Both men wore Burberry trench coats, and plaid mufflers were wrapped tightly across their chests. Joseph held his gloves in his left hand and took Arla's hand in his right: "Arla," he said. "Leon has been singing your praises all the way up the Hudson. He says the museum would fall apart without you." Joseph's voice was nasal and flat, his accent hard to define. He didn't sound as though he came from the East, but from far away.

"Where is Monique?" Leon asked. "Late, as usual?"

"Let me take your coats," Arla said. "We'll put them right here in the cloakroom. Monique isn't late. She won't be coming and sends her regrets. The plane couldn't land because of the snow."

"Typical, I might say. A plane for this trip."

Arla led the visitors to the central room of the museum, and Leon said, "We will proceed without her. You are wondering why I've brought an architect."

"A little." With Joseph and Leon, Arla looked at the surrounding rooms. The floors were bare pine boards, waxed and polished. There was an Oriental rug in one of the smaller rooms, but that was the only floor covering. The walls were plaster, painted a white selected by Monique, and the ceilings were a lighter shade of white. Perhaps because he was an architect, Joseph Bird seemed to look at the rooms and the building from a greater distance than Leon or Arla, accepting nothing as given or permanent, not the walls or the ceilings that had been there for over a hundred years, nor the shape of the building itself. He had green eyes, which made Arla think of a proverb: Blue eyes say, "Love me or I'll die." Brown eyes say, "Love me or I'll kill you." She'd always thought the choice between brown eyes and blue eyes was a bad one.

"It isn't so certain what Joseph will do," said Leon. "So we will tell you only when the day is over. This young man has his practice in Boston, Arla, and knows very well the value of buildings."

"Like the John Hancock," Arla said.

"As one example," said Joseph.

"Would you like coffee or tea?" she asked. "This weather makes us all so cold." But the two men preferred to walk

through the museum. At Leon's request, Arla showed them
through the exhibition rooms, the storage space, her office.
When they discussed what had been done to the original
house, she added that she had kept working while the back
of the museum was being gutted to create the double-storied
storage and office space. She was then ripping down the
cracked plaster walls of her own house—a vernacular house,
she told them, but perhaps older than the museum—and she'd
gone from bomb site to bomb site. She never discussed anything personal with Monique or Leon, and Arla felt she'd
forced herself on the two men. Joseph took in her comment
with as much neutrality as he did the information he re-
quested from her: statistics on heating bills, humidifying,
number of visitors, and any needs she felt for more space,
more storage room, or, he suggested, for a more presentable
office. "I wouldn't mind," she said. "I spend a lot of time in
the office, after all, and there isn't even room really for the
files. I hate to take up storage space, though."

"You have mentioned this to Monique?" asked Leon.

"It's not a real problem," she answered. She had mentioned
it to both Monique and Leon, but they'd forgotten.

They had lunch a few miles down the highway at a restaurant that had been converted from a gambrel-roofed cow
barn. The genuinely old timbers were exposed and the newly
created walls covered with rough plaster. They were seated at
a round table near a stone fireplace of baronial proportions.
Arla thought Leon looked older and tired. Through lunch he
questioned her about the museum and told her about shows
he'd seen that season in New York and Europe. She wondered
what they would have been talking about if Monique had been
there, if she would have been given his attention at all. While
they drank their coffee, Arla and Joseph talked generally
about Boston, then went on to see if they had any mutual
friends in that city or New York. When Arla looked over at
Leon, she saw that he was asleep, his chin on his chest.

"I wish I could fall asleep like that," Joseph said.

"He does that during meetings. Sometimes."

"I didn't think we were that dull."

"Just irrelevant. He's made up his mind about something and he's ready to move on."

"It's a wonderful family to work with," said Joseph. "In that way at least. They leave you alone once they've given you the job."

"Someone once said that Monique nodded when you spoke to her, to reassure you she was still alive," Arla said. It was indiscreet to say that, she knew. She wondered if Joseph and Monique were having an affair or if it was business. She knew nothing about Monique's life except that she'd been married twice, once to an Italian, once to a Frenchman, a distant cousin. The sleeping man and snow drew Arla and Joseph together, and she wanted to know more about him. "What's the secret?" she asked. "Why are you here?"

"It isn't my secret. It's Leon's. He'll tell you soon enough."

The waitress woke Leon when she asked if they wanted anything more. He stirred himself; once his eyes were open, he was awake. "We must be going," he said. "The check, if you please." He went over the addition and handed the waitress a credit card. He tapped his pen against the tablecloth. "It is unfortunate after all that Monique isn't here."

"Is there something I can do?" Arla asked.

"There is no need to be so evasive," Leon said, and he smiled briefly. His eyes were a pale blue—Love me or I'll die. "The museum is at a new point, Arla. My eldest sister died recently in Amsterdam and left her entire collection to Monique."

"Her collection?"

"The De Nuys glass collection."

She'd heard of it; it was the best collection of glass in the world, not only as a comprehensive sampling of techniques and periods, but for its aesthetic merit as well. The collection ranged from Roman bottles to early industrial glassware, and included figurines, crystal bowls and chandeliers, goblets, vases, statuettes. As far as Arla could recall, the collection— the work of forty years' searching and buying by Madame de

Nuys—had never been cataloged or exhibited as a whole. Most important decorative-arts shows included a piece or two borrowed from the collection. Arla hadn't known Madame de Nuys was Leon's sister. His family was a mystery to her, from the extent of their fortune to their motivation in spending it as they did. Once when she'd been doing research in New York, Arla had lunch with a curator at the Metropolitan, who told her that Monique's mother, now long dead, had been a student of art at the Boston Museum School. She was American, heiress to another great fortune, which was now Monique's.

"Will we show the whole collection here?" Arla asked. "What a coup."

"More than a coup," Leon said. "We've suspected this would come for a while, Arla, and considered simply handing over the collection to the Louvre or the Metropolitan—more people would see it, obviously. But it is ours to do with what we like, and the museum will become prominent through this gift. Scholars will come to visit and to study. The collection will be on permanent display. In its own glass wing. That is, if Joseph agrees that it can be done. Monique will organize the move from Amsterdam and the first show."

"I think the wing will work," Joseph said. "We've been thinking of a separate building, Arla, leading up to a complex of buildings perhaps, but Monique and I agree that it would preserve the integrity of the museum as it stands, for the glass wing to be a part of the original building."

Arla leaned back in her chair. The administration of such a collection was a task as large as hers in the present museum. What would the collection do to her job? Would Monique bring in an outside expert or expect her to take care of the glass collection as well?

"When will this happen?" Arla asked.

"The wing will go up as soon as possible," said Leon. "How soon, this is up to Joseph Bird. We could have a show next fall, perhaps, would you say, Joseph?"

"That isn't far off the mark. If we can agree on the design

before mid-April, groundbreaking could take place then. It's a relatively simple project. It could be closed in before summer." Joseph lit a thin cigar and leaned back in his chair to blow out a thin stream of smoke. Somehow his gesture settled Arla. "That's amazing," she said. "So soon."

"You are in charge of Joseph," Leon said. "He will not be here every single minute, so he will not disturb your work. For the time being, everything is the same. The landscape show can proceed, and the show of circus posters. But he should be here as long and as often as he needs."

"When will you start?" Arla asked.

Joseph smiled at her. "I've started already. I'm going back to New York now, then to Boston. I'll be back." He reached into his pocket and gave her his card, black lettering on thin white paper.

"So," said Leon, "the matter is settled."

A few hours later, Arla drove them to the train. She told Bob to close up when he felt like going home. The roads looked bad, and no one would come to the museum in this weather. She knew he'd keep the museum open until closing time, more strict than she in his sense of public duty. Maybe someone would struggle up the driveway to stand in a white room looking at a pastel of red peonies.

Along the way, Joseph pointed out classical architecture and hot-dog stands. He admired a large cemetery outside of Troy in which there were no stones or monuments visible through the snow, only evenly placed bouquets of plastic flowers. "I wonder what I'll push up," Joseph said. "I hope it isn't plastic flowers."

"Glass buildings, maybe," Arla said.

"What is the saying about glass houses?" Leon asked.

"If you live in a glass house," said Joseph, "don't throw rocks."

"That's a strange saying," Arla said. "Does that mean that most people want to break their own houses?"

"It's probably a form of architectural criticism," Joseph

said. "Or just more direct times."

"Poor Troy," Leon said. "This must have been once an industrial center. One can see that."

"It was filled with marvelous examples of brickwork," Joseph said. "I did a study of Troy when I was at Yale. The city's nearly destroyed now."

The ruins of Troy were hard to drive. Once they had crossed the Hudson on the Green Island Bridge and driven along 787, the trip to the station was almost over. Arla would get them to the 5:20 train with no problem. She wanted to stay with them on the train to New York. They would open doors for her and offer her a drink from the dining car. She wanted to be in the padded train with them, watching snow fall on the Hudson.

"Here we are," she said.

The train station was in a large empty lot on one side of which was a Pricechopper supermarket and a Pricechopper gas station. Both the Pricechopper and the cashier's booth by the gas pumps were prefabricated metal. There was a view across the river of the new skyscrapers in Albany and of the railroad yard. There weren't enough tracks for the yard to look romantic, despite snow and a steaming train. Arla stopped her car in front of the train station.

"This station doesn't make any sense," said Joseph.

"It is no place," Leon said. "A train station should be in the heart of a city."

"A little bit of Americana," Arla said. "Don't be too hard on it—it's the only place we've got to catch a train."

"Come in with us for a drink," Joseph said. "There's time before the train."

"There's no bar in there. And I should get home."

"It's true," Leon said. "You have a drive in the snow. Well, bon voyage to us all. Monique will be in touch with you. So will Joseph."

"Will you be back for the circus show?" she asked.

"I am going to Egypt. I've meant to go for so long and have been prevented before. This time, I shall go no matter what. I shall spend some time with the pyramids and in the Cairo

museum. Then I will continue to go where I like. Since the
telephone, it is all so simple."

"I'll call," Joseph said. "Take it easy driving."

Taking it easy was just what it was impossible to do. The
news announced travelers' advisories for all roads, and rush
hour was just beginning. Arla reached Troy by 5:10, and the
streets were worse than they'd been a half hour before. The
Christmas decorations strung along lampposts, hanging limp
and ugly, reminded Arla it was bad luck to leave them up
beyond the new year. Back at the cemetery on Route 40 Arla
noticed that the snow had piled up since she'd driven by with
Joseph and Leon. The car seemed light without the two men.
She had noticed the road when they were with her, though it
was a landscape driven before and ignored a long time hence.

Her lights picked up every flake, and it was only because
she could have driven blind that she was able to guide herself
along the familiar curves. She saw cows and horses standing
in the snow, their backs covered with a layer of white, and a
cat ran across her path by a clump of trailers a few miles from
her house. She was thinking of what she would have for dinner—soup, bread she'd baked that weekend—when she saw a
car by the side of the road. Its lights were fading, its back
end stuck up in the air. If it had been summer, she might have
passed by. Sometimes kids parked, though not usually on such
an open road. She pulled up in back of the car and walked
over to it. There was an old man slumped in the driver's seat
and what looked like a bundle of clothes on the seat beside
him. The doors were locked and the windows closed. Arla
tapped on the window and asked, "Are you all right?"

"For God's sake," the old man said. "Get somebody. It's
her."

"Your doors are locked," Arla said.

"Get somebody," he said. "Never mind about me."

She tried the door again and then thought: what could she
do if she did get it open? The bundle of clothes was a woman.
"I'll go for help," Arla said. "I'll be back as soon as I can."

Half a mile up the road was a large horse farm. The owners lived in Rochester and came there only six weeks a year, but the caretaker was always there. The snow was newly shoveled in a path leading to the back door of his house. The house was fairly new and shaped like an ark. The only windows were high up, at the level of the roof, so that, unlike most houses, it was impossible to see in or out of it. Arla knocked on the glass storm door, then rang the doorbell, but the wind obscured the knocking and she couldn't hear the bell. She tried the storm door, but it was locked. If the caretaker weren't home, she would have to go up the hill to her own house to use the phone; there were no other houses between hers and the horse farm. She knocked again and rang the bell, but still there was no answer. Arla waited, and as she was about to leave, the inner door opened and the caretaker stood looking at her through the glass door.

"I'm Arla Stein," she said. She had to shout to reach above the noise of the wind. "I live up the road. There's been an accident on Railroad Bed."

"Just a minute," the caretaker said, and he closed the door. When he reappeared, he was wearing a jacket over workpants and a pajama top. "Cold night," he said, and opened the storm door a crack.

"There's a man in the car," Arla said. "And a woman. They're both badly hurt."

"Any idea who it is?" he asked.

"No. Can I use your phone to call the Rescue Squad?" When he didn't answer, she said, "Or you could call."

"Sure," he said. "If you think they're the ones to call. The state police need to know when there's an accident. Any kind of car accident, that is."

"Or the police," Arla said. "Or both."

"I could call the Rescue Squad," he said. "They can call the police. You might as well come in while I call. Then we'll go out there."

The snow on her jacket melted as soon as she stepped into the warm house. The air smelled of sleep and cabbage. He'd been fast asleep, Arla realized. It was six o'clock and dark and there was no reason why he shouldn't have been sleeping. Arla thought of herself on the road every morning and evening, counting fences and cows, watching the sun fade. This man didn't leave the property, went to bed at six. When she woke he'd probably been up for hours. He dialed the number slowly, looking back after each digit at the orange sticker on his wall phone on which the numbers of the volunteer fire department and the Rescue Squad were printed. When the caretaker reached the Rescue Squad, he told them there'd been an accident on Railroad Bed. "How far along?" he asked Arla, and she told him it was a half mile or so above Easton Station; he repeated this information and then hung up.

"They'll be here," he said. "As soon as they can."

"Will they call the police?"

"Couldn't tell you," he said. "I'll put on my things."

He laced his boots slowly and carefully. She thought of the old man in the car. The laces finally finished, his jacket buttoned, hat firm on his head, gloves in his hands, they left the house and walked along the path to her car.

"Seems a shame to use the car for such a short walk," he said.

"I might as well take it," Arla said. "I'm trying to get home."

"Suit yourself," said the caretaker. "I'll walk, myself."

Nothing had changed in the car. The old man said again, "For God's sake. Get somebody."

"It's me again," Arla said. "The Rescue Squad is coming." She felt she was shouting into the land of the dead, where the words "Rescue Squad" meant nothing. "He must be freezing," she said when the caretaker walked up beside her.

"We could get him out of there," the caretaker said. He didn't reach for the door or touch the window.

"The glass would have to be broken," Arla said. The windshield on the passenger side had already been smashed, but that was with the woman's head. "Better to leave him," she said, though she wanted to do something. "He'll just get colder out here. We don't know what's broken." They stood in the cold, waiting for the ambulance. She couldn't think of anything to say either to the caretaker or to the man in the car. He had probably forgotten they were there. The caretaker was looking around, though there wasn't much to see but snow in the woods and snow on the road. Arla was wearing boots that were too thin to stand up to the weather; her feet were wet and cold by now. She could go home, she thought. She couldn't do anything more for anyone. She could wait in her car, she thought; but she stayed outside, feeling colder and wetter. The bundle of clothes didn't move.

The lights of the Rescue Squad made a red glow in the snow, the police car made blue. Arla backed up her own car so that they could get closer to the accident, then remained in her car. The caretaker walked over and stood by the car. Together they watched the ambulance and the police car park and let out their passengers. Someone had a crowbar and used it on the doors of the car; then the doors of the ambulance blocked Arla's view of the accident. A policeman with an unlit flare in his hand walked back to Arla's car.

"Bad accident," said the caretaker.

The trooper looked sick. "Don't go up there," he said. He spoke to Arla. "Don't go to that car. There's a dead woman in that car."

She had seen the car, she wanted to say, and didn't know what there was left to fear, but she felt frightened. The trooper continued down the road and lit the flare. He tried to stake it in the frozen ground, and failing, propped it in a snowbank. Arla started her engine and turned on her headlight.

"Do you want a ride home?" she asked the caretaker.

"Nope," he said. "Might as well stay here."

"Good night," Arla said, and she drove away past the ambulance and the accident, up the hill to her house. When she reached home, she looked back down the hill. She expected to see reflections of lights from the cars gathered on Railroad Bed, but she saw only the lights strung along the ski trails miles past the accident. The mountain always looked festive to her on winter nights, a party that went on without her. The accident vanished, though afterward when she passed that spot on Railroad Bed, Arla always turned her head to look where the car had been, as if a dead woman should have left some trace.

In the morning, Arla had a sore throat. She could feel the infection rise from her throat to her ears, and she settled in to be sick. There were two storms that week, one after the other. The power went out for forty minutes, just long enough for Arla to light the kerosene lamps, stoke the fire in the wood stove, move her thermometer, teacup, books, and pillow from her bedroom to the back room. Then the lights and the furnace came back on.

The second storm was worse than the first, throwing snow against the windows in lumps. Snow came from underneath the foundation, blown upward by the violent wind, and Arla wondered if the snow would somehow penetrate the electric wires and cause a fire. But nothing happened. The snow melted on the floor by the next morning.

Once the snowplows had come and gone on Friday morning, Arla drove into town to see a doctor whose name she got out of the Yellow Pages. His office was around the back of an old yellow-brick building; the waiting room was decorated with framed magazine covers by Norman Rockwell of country doctors and their patients. The doctor gave her white envelopes of antibiotics and antihistamines; then she went to the grocery store and stocked up. She bought vegetables and eggs, more butter and milk, a *TV Guide*, a box of pretzels, and two six-packs of ginger ale. She bought a lime because she was surprised to see it in March. She used all the cash she had with her to pay for her groceries, and the discovery that she had the exact amount down to the penny made her feel sure of everything. The sky was clear as she drove home, the patterns of snow set in the fields. Arla put the car away, carried in wood for a few days, fed the cats, and fell asleep. When she woke, it was dark. People had said all that fall that it would be a closed winter, and Arla had liked the sound of the phrase. Now she thought the words were only the bare truth.

By Saturday she was getting better and was bored with thinking. She listened to a morning music-show broadcast from Boston, and when the weather in Boston was announced as sunny but cold, Arla thought of Joseph Bird. He probably lived in a town house in Back Bay, in an apartment furnished sparsely with Eames chairs and a round white Formica table from Milan. That night she had trouble sleeping, and woke at two in the morning. She sat up in the cold house and saw her situation as ridiculous. She was a young woman, buried in the country. Things weighed too heavily on her, she was not living the life she could; she was lonely, trapped. Arla considered turning on the bedroom light, getting up and making another cup of tea. She thought of moving into the back room and reading the last unread article in an old magazine, then finally fell back to sleep.

On Sunday afternoon Arla sat in the heavy red armchair by the wood stove and looked the length of her house—fifty feet end to end. In summer when the front door stayed open, Arla could see all the way across the dead-end road and her neighbor's fields. Sometimes she doubted it had really been her mother's house. She'd seen it only a few times when she was much younger, and the house was ordinary in itself. Once in a while she took the deed from her desk drawer and stared at her mother's name on it as if that would tell her something beyond dates and boundaries. No one local remembered her mother. She'd only been there weekends and had died in the city. Now she was buried in Queens and Arla never went to the grave. One year after her mother's death, she'd returned with her mother's friend for the unveiling. Since that time, her mother had been left in Queens.

She'd lost her mother twice, once through death, once before that, when Arla was seven and they moved from Brooklyn to Manhattan. The move preceded the divorce by only a few months, and seemed in retrospect worse than when her fa-

ther left them. Her mother told her they were moving because they needed more space, but Arla had always imagined
that the apartment in Brooklyn had more space. She imagined
a room that extended from their living room, though when
she looked out the living-room window, she saw the windows
and roofs of the neighboring houses and the little yards of
Brooklyn Heights, not another room. Now she could not quite
remember if this was true, for it seemed neater than most
memories, but Arla remembered that in the move they had
forgotten all her stuffed animals and dolls. It had been a
nightly ritual in Brooklyn Heights for her to take the dolls and
animals—twenty, thirty, more—off the bed one by one and lay
them on the floor in the same place every night. She would
prop up the dolls and animals, one by one, friends close by,
get into her own bed, and fall asleep. She used to sleep with
all of them on the bed with her, but her mother asked her to
stop and so she had. When they left Brooklyn, her parents left
her dolls and animals behind, or so Arla remembered. There
wasn't anyone to ask about it. Her father never liked remembering, and her mother was dead. Perhaps her mother had decided it was time for Arla to give up dolls and she'd taken advantage of the move to get rid of them. Yet Arla felt that the
mother who had been her mother was left behind with the
missing dolls. The mother in Manhattan worked in an office
and picked Arla up at a play group at five every day. She was
a person who talked to Arla, talked as she walked her to the
bus stop in the morning, as she took her grocery shopping in
the winter evenings, took her downtown Saturday and late
Thursday nights for bargains at S. Klein's. She talked to her
all the time, but what had she told Arla? Arla couldn't remember. Something must have gotten into Arla's head, for she
had all the prejudices of her mother—use Tide for the wash
and Ivory for the bath, oil a floor this way, never buy things
like Twinkies and Hostess cupcakes with cream at the center.

The entire length of Arla's house—all she could see from
her red armchair—represented her work on the house. She had
patched old plaster and torn down walls damaged beyond re-

pair. She'd put up plasterboard and had spent whatever money she had on carpenters to make doorways into walls, to add a new window in the back room. From the outside, the finished downstairs and unfinished upstairs looked the same, but the upstairs had been stripped of plaster and lath. In the shells of rooms, Arla stored her boxes of papers, photographs, old clothing, dishes, abandoned knitting and sewing projects. One day she would clear it out. She planned to finish one upstairs bedroom that summer and made passes upstairs at the changing of the seasons, throwing away a little something, giving something else away.

Arla still dreamed of the apartment in Brooklyn with its extra room, and her dreams expanded to include dreams of additional rooms in her present house, rooms abandoned full of furniture and goods, open drawers full of laces and petticoats, cabinets of china and glass, all someone else's goods, the owner dead or absent. In her dreams, Arla was in charge of the goods; it was her task to separate what she wanted from what she could discard. She was struck by the richness and variety of the rooms. In one dream there was a Viennese turn-of-the-century parlor, in another a pioneer kitchen in the Far West. The dream rooms were reached through the upstairs of her houses. When she finished the upstairs, Arla wondered, where would the additional rooms go?

It snowed again on Sunday night, and Arla worried that she wouldn't be able to go to work the next day. When Monday morning came, she was surprised to see that it was beautiful. After the storms of the past weeks, the sun was strong. By the time she was dressed for work, the snowplow had come and gone, and Arla could see her week as clearly as she could the road away from home—she would catch up on the missed work, call Monique, perhaps go to New York for the afternoon to see her. She would start to learn about glass. As she left the bedroom, she noticed her socks from the day before on the floor, and before she picked them up, she looked at them with tenderness as if they were living things she was fond of. The sight of her own socks lying around sometimes

reassured her that she was present; at other times she saw
such piles as artifacts of another person, someone dead or
absent. She wanted to stay in the bedroom, unmake the bed,
go back to sleep. Her mother had taught her by example never
to leave a kitchen dirty to face the next morning or a bed unmade for the night. Now Arla thought: Why did everything
have to be so nice, why did everything have to be done right?
She wondered if her mother had as hard a time as she getting
through her days. She couldn't remember—she only recalled
the making of beds, the cleaning of floors, the pattern in the
living-room rug after her mother vacuumed. There was seren-
ity in the living room after cleaning. The room waited intact
for Arla to return from school, her father from work. The living room was a Brooklyn memory, one that had taken place
before the move to Manhattan, the divorce and cancer. Arla
remembered the days of her mother's illness as the idleness of
her mother's hands more than the wasting of the rest of her
mother. She wondered if in the last days in the hospital, her
mother thought of unmade beds and unfinished rooms, or if
she traveled back to Brooklyn in the early days. She wondered
if her mother remembered things she never told Arla.

Once Arla had cleared her own hill, the day opened up.
Winter was now not an obstacle but the whole point of the
landscape. The situation of the houses, the fences rising from
the snowdrifts, the deep blue sky, couldn't have been better.
The scene settled Arla. She couldn't live in a better place. She
remembered thinking another morning on the way to work
that things couldn't be very bad if she continued to bake her
own bread. She tried to recall what she had been so slow about
all week, why she'd dragged herself around as she had. She'd
been sick, she thought, and when you're sick your thoughts
are slow and old. She looked at the museum as her car climbed
the drive. She couldn't imagine what the glass wing would
look like. She could only imagine something like a glass sun-
porch tacked on to the back of the building.

Arla unlocked the front door and walked into the museum.
Morning light shone into the central hall from every direction.

Whoever had designed the building had meant it for this Monday in March. The sound of the waxer meant Bob must have started in the East Room. She crossed the entrance hall into the area marked "Private," and from across the storage area she saw into her office. On the desk was a pile of mail and phone messages. As she closed the office door behind her, Arla heard the furnace click on—winter.

By taking an early-morning train into New York, Arla was able to spend most of the day with Monique and return home on the four-thirty train. It was a Turboliner, upholstered and carpeted in colors she didn't like. She chose a seat on the river side and watched the sun set gradually over the Hudson as the train moved upstate. The meeting had been productive. All the papers she'd brought were spread out over the parquet floor in the drawing room, and Arla doubted they would finish in one day; by the end of the afternoon, it had all been taken care of. Monique worked fast, not looking back at decisions. Driving home from the train station in Rensselaer, Arla thought for the first time that she could have stayed in the city, had dinner with her father or a friend from the publishing house who still sent Arla books and an occasional letter urging Arla to call when she was in the city. She could have stayed overnight perhaps. She was troubled, not so much because she'd missed a pleasant evening but because it hadn't occurred to her to do anything but see Monique, turn around, and come back home. By the time she reached her house, it was almost nine. Her dishes from breakfast were still in the sink. She poured a glass of red wine and drank it while she did the dishes. When she'd eaten a piece of bread and drunk another glass of wine, she was just as glad she'd come home. She was tired, she didn't like being in the city, and there was too much to do to stay away on an impulse.

Joseph Bird called the museum the next morning to say he would be there the next day. He arrived around lunchtime in a car Arla thought at first was a Mercedes. It turned out to be a Volvo. The passenger side was pushed in—not his fault, he

said—and when he took her to dinner that night, Arla had to
climb in on the driver's side. She gave him blueprints of the
original renovation and measured floor plans of the museum.
Snow was falling thickly, but Joseph took his camera, screwed
on a wide-angle lens, and went outside. He walked slowly
around the museum in widening circles, moving farther away
until he was at the bottom of the drive, almost on the highway, and all Arla could see of him was the band of interna-
tional orange on his camera strap.

"Maybe he's using infrared film," Bob said.

"Maybe he doesn't know what he's doing," Arla said, but
she didn't believe that. Joseph Bird would always know what
he was doing—she'd known that about him from the minute
she saw him. He came back inside the museum covered with
snow. His glasses clouded in the heated air, and when he took
them off to rub them clear, Arla saw again his green eyes.

"Nice weather you've got up here," he said. "Does it always
snow?"

"Just in winter," Arla said. "Did your walk give you any
ideas for the wing?"

"Not yet. But I'll come up with a design in a week. This is
a rush operation, you know."

"Hurry up and wait. Don't always believe Monique's dead-
lines. She sets them more as optimistic goals."

"Oh, I have to believe her," Joseph said. "On the off-chance
the client is consistent, it would be fatal for the architect to
slip up."

Joseph spent the rest of the day at a large table Bob set up
for him in the storage space. The table was a piece of Masonite
resting on sawhorses. Joseph unrolled the blueprints and floor
plans and weighted down the ends of the drawings with some
iron banks in the shape of trains, boats, houses. He looked
right in the storage space, Arla thought as she passed him on
her way from one task to another. She worked that day on the
schedule for the rest of the year, up to the completion of the
wing and the opening of the glass show. In New York, she and
Monique had set a rough schedule, and now Arla worked in

the times for shipping, hanging, publicity, openings, closings. Until the glass show they would have a watercolor-landscape show by a local artist, a show of circus posters from the Ringling Museum in Sarasota, Florida, and in the fall photographs of American barns by an aged German expressionist painter, a friend of Leon's. Arla and Bob were having coffee in her office, trying to decide how many rooms they would have to clear for the circus show, when Joseph walked in and stood at the window, looking out at the snow. Arla felt self-conscious talking in front of him, and she ended the discussion sooner than she would have liked. Afterward, she thought he probably could have helped them if he'd wanted, trained as he was in spatial arrangements. Or perhaps he hadn't been listening to them at all, and was absorbed in thinking of the glass wing.

"Flexibility," Joseph said at dinner. "That's what most people think is good architecture. That's what most people demand from architecture."

"And life," said Arla.

"I wouldn't know about that," he said. "In my experience, people settle for whatever safety they can find. But in architecture, perfectly nice people, once they've decided they want an architect to design for them, demand maximum flexibility. The impossible. In the case of this glass wing, for instance, Monique wants a space designed especially for this collection —which I haven't seen and which she doesn't seem to have an inventory for—and also to make the space modular for later expansion. She wants more office space for the enlarged staff, not to be built now, or maybe yes. She wants walls and windows in the same space."

"The enlarged staff?"

"A curator for the glass," he said. "I couldn't be sure if she meant it. The offices are low on the list of priorities."

"I'll hear about it soon enough," Arla said. "I guess."

"It's the old problem of wanting things both ways. Shall we look at the menus?"

They ordered veal and mushrooms, agreed to share a half-bottle of red wine. He asked if she'd grown up in the area, and when she told him she was from New York, he looked surprised. "You don't seem like a New Yorker," he said. She told him she'd left the city over three years before, and he took in the information, not asking her, as did most people, why she'd come to the country.

"Are you from the Midwest?" she asked. "I can't tell by your accent."

"I grew up in Texas," he said, "Oklahoma, Louisiana. But I went to high school in Galveston and I think of Galveston as home. I think that's where I decided to be an architect, looking at the old railings and fences, all those Victorian houses."

"Where's Galveston in Texas?"

"Right on the Gulf of Mexico," Joseph said, and he smiled. "Right on the water. I thought of staying in Texas. I went to UT in Austin and could have gone to architecture school there, but I figured if I didn't come East right away, later would be too late." He'd chosen Yale over MIT because he thought it was better for design, but he'd hated New Haven. "My life would have been different if I'd been in Boston all those years," he said, but he was smiling and Arla couldn't tell if places made that much difference to Joseph. "I moved to Boston right away when I graduated, and worked for Urban Architecture long enough to get registered. And then I went out on my own. In the middle of the worst recession in decades."

"And how's business?" Arla asked.

"Not wonderful. This commission is the most exciting thing that's happened in a long time. I met Monique in California, when I was doing a rehab on an old Spanish house for a cousin of hers. Monique's been talking about this museum for years. Sometimes these things work out, sometimes they don't. I mean, work themselves into a project that really happens."

"And do you still like Boston?"

"I have a view of Richardson's church and the public library from my bedroom. I like Boston well enough. Still."

As Arla drove home that night, the snow-covered barns

and houses looked crude to her. People built houses to keep the snow and the rain off their heads. Then they refined from there. Arla felt proud of the porches. They were manifestations of easier times, indicating additional room for additional leisure. The porches on the farmhouses were the party hats of the buildings. Her whole idea of houses was changed by talking to Joseph.

On his second visit, they had dinner again. She invited him to come home with her for dinner, but he refused, saying he'd take her out. Bob had gone home early and the office was peaceful. "Too much trouble for you," Joseph said. "After working all day."

"It's no trouble," she said. "I like to cook."

"But it's so easy in restaurants. You can get whatever you want. I'd live in a hotel if I had the money. Anyway, we're three minutes from that restaurant we ate in last time."

"You must think I'm a bad cook," she said. Now, almost the end of March, it had rained for three days and was threatening to clear. The small sun was reflected in the puddles on the museum lawn.

"No," Joseph said. "I'm sure you're a wonderful cook. It's the time, Arla. There just isn't the time."

Arla figured he had a girlfriend or a wife in Boston, but she didn't ask him. She didn't want to know too much about him, as if further knowledge would lay claim to him or lead her to hope for something that might not happen.


"Arla," said Monique. "Are we still connected?"

"I was just thinking. That's awfully tight, isn't it? An opening of the wing before Christmas is sooner than it seems. I mean, can we do it?"

"The architect is here with me." Monique whispered: "Yes. That phone. There," and then Joseph's voice: "I'm on the line, too, Arla."

"Good. Hello. Well, now that we're all here. I still think it's tight. I don't know anything about building, but for selecting objects to be shown, and the shipping, and you want an exten-

sive, accurate catalog, don't you, Monique? The editing, pho-
tography, printing, and binding all take time."

"It is nearly a year until next December. The photographs
can be taken *in situ* in Amsterdam and the plates made there
as well. I am committing myself to this show. Completely. I
am not alone in this estimate. I have discussed this with curators here in New York. It is not at all out of the question.
There are several scholars in line for the catalog. The curator-
ship of the collection also. When I find the right person, we
shall begin sending you material to edit. I see no problems,
Arla. You will hold up this end. It isn't as if there were not
telephones."

"No," said Arla. "It isn't."

Monique said, "The excavations begin as soon as the ground
is soft enough."

Arla looked out the window at the muddy lawn and the
driveway with its two tracks of mud. "When will that be?"

"Soon," Joseph said. "I'm winding up negotiations with the
contractors up there. As soon as that's set, we get going."

Monique's voice changed now. "I've approved the design.
Marvelous. What potential. What light there will be." Arla
was trying to be friendly but heard herself saying, "Yes. Like
a greenhouse," and she thought of steam forming on glass.
She and Monique discussed more details and the new schedule
Arla had mailed her two weeks before. She thought she heard
a click at one point but wasn't sure; Joseph Bird didn't say
anything more for the rest of the conversation. When the call
ended, Arla walked out into the museum area. Bob was in his
favorite room, polishing a window.

"I just spoke to Monique," Arla said.

"How's our leader?"

"O.K. We won't be seeing her for a while—how long, who
knows? She's going to Amsterdam to collect the glass collection. We'll communicate with those overseas calls. Longer
pauses than usual."

"You don't sound too thrilled about it."

"It's a lot of work for me. A lot of responsibility. You

know, she's getting a curator for the collection. Someone trained, unlike myself."

"Your job's safe, Arla. This place wouldn't last five minutes without you."

"I don't know. Even if that's true, I don't know if she thinks so. I have the feeling something's going to happen. She's even going to build the curator a new office."

"Who's going to supervise Frank Lloyd Wright if Monique's in Amsterdam and Leon's in Cairo?"

"I guess he'll supervise himself. Don't you like him?"

"He's all right." Bob sat beside her on the leather couch Monique had donated to the museum when she redecorated her New York living room. "I mean," Bob said, "why is he hanging around so much?"

"He's doing his job, isn't he?"

"No, Arla. An architect takes pictures, elevations, measures, draws. It's mostly on paper, and then the building starts. My brother-in-law's an architect in Glens Falls, and I asked him. The guy's been here three times now. There's no reason for that."

"Maybe he wants to soak up the atmosphere. He's attaching something new to something old. I think it's good that he wants to see the old building."

"I wonder what he wants out of Monique."

"Monique?"

"It would be handy for an architect to have a zillionaire in his pocket."

"That hadn't occurred to me."

"You're too nice," said Bob.

Arla watched TV that night and mended a cotton summer dress. The material felt flimsy in her hands. Summer would never come. Mud would stay. Her lawn was torn up by cars going in and out when friends visited and she went to work. It was a dreary season and she felt nothing new would ever happen. Her circle was closed. She would spend Saturday nights for the rest of her life having dinner with the same people: the Potters, who taught at Skidmore; Karl and Clara, both painters, who lived in the woods near Bob and stretched Clara's trust fund as far as they could; Annie, whose husband had left in the fall and who was thinking of leaving herself. The food was always wonderful, everything made from scratch, and at the best moments—everyone seated, the table looking beautiful, knowing her friends through years of different seasons, problems—Arla felt that she was in the right place. But it was damning evidence of the smallness of her life that she would entertain fancies about Joseph Bird. She tried to specify what she liked about him, but it came to her disconnected—his eyes; the way he wore his clothes simply, like a uniform; his voice, sounding only faintly of Texas; the shape of his hands. There was something weak about his lower lip. He made quiet jokes. She wondered if he was really a good architect or if, like her, he was someone Monique had picked up and decided to try out—a way of saving money perhaps, a way of keeping things in her control. The new curator would be trained for work in a museum. It would become evident as time went on that Arla had invented procedures, systems, that she did not know how to run a museum out of anything but her own experience in doing it. She had been waiting to lose her job since she'd been given it; it was as unlikely that she would keep it as that she would ever have found it. If she liked a person for the color of his eyes or the shape of his hands, then what accurate clues existed to tell her what he was like? The next time Joseph Bird came, she would tell him she couldn't have dinner. She wanted sure things in her life. If the sure things, like her house, were not always responsive, that was all right too. Before she went to sleep, she thought of being alone and content the week she'd been sick in March. She thought of it as her safe time and realized she hadn't appreciated it enough. She never appreciated things as they happened; that was the trouble.

Joseph Bird phoned at the museum a few days later. "It's time to start the excavation," he said. "I've settled things rather quickly with the contractors. The papers are all going through. Excavation begins April twentieth. In that week."

Arla looked at her desk calendar. "That's a Wednesday."

"I'll be there the twelfth and then pretty much stay around full time."

"Don't you have any other jobs?" she asked.

"Don't you want me around?" When she didn't answer, he said, "Well?"

"That's not the point."

"I'll be there in a few days. Will you reserve my room at the motel? Same room, same motel."

"I don't know which room you had."

"The motel-keeper will."

She should have asked him a lot of questions. How would the construction affect the museum? What did she and Bob have to do to get ready, if anything? He had never promised her anything or made an advance toward her. He probably wanted nothing from her. The point was, people could feel these things, could tell where there was more than business. Most people could, but she couldn't, as if her antennae were atrophied from lack of use or of trust.

The twelfth was a real spring day. The air smelled different, not only of wet earth but of green shoots, and it was warm enough so that Arla didn't have to use the heat in her car. She reached the museum before Bob, and the phone was ringing as she unlocked the door. She let it ring while she turned off the alarm system, then ran for it.

"Arla? At last. I've been trying for hours."

"I just got to work, Monique. I was just opening the door when the phone rang." There was a pause for the words to reach Monique in Amsterdam. Monique always sounded more cheerful in Europe.

"In any case," said Monique, "there you are. How is it at the museum?"

"Well, I've seen proofs of the invitations for the circus show. That will open the twenty-seventh of May, Memorial Day weekend. The posters should arrive on schedule, no problem. The watercolors are up—they don't take up more than one room, after all. I think we can get that circus school up for the day from New York, as we discussed. The director said that if I chartered a bus and provided food and drink for the clowns and acrobats, they'd be happy to come. I thought we should make a small contribution to the school as well."

"Fine. All that is fine. Arla, I have an important task for you. This is in connection with the glass show."

"All right." Arla moved a yellow pad closer to her and got a pen to write down what Monique had to say. "I'm ready."

"I have been discussing the show with several very qualified people here and in Paris. They are enthusiastic about the show. But one person in particular who is a very talented man, an old friend of my aunt's, he suggests there is one piece that should not be left out, even though it is not part of the collection. An American piece."

"That makes sense."

"One doesn't always think of these things. The piece—are you writing this down?—is owned by a Mr. and Mrs. Peter Unterecker. They live in some place in Vermont. Montpelier."

"Montpeelier."

"What a terrible way to pronounce the name. However. He teaches somewhere. The piece was made in New England and given to his father-in-law by some eccentric."

"What kind of piece is it?" Arla thought of a glass eagle.

"It sounds marvelous. There is one rather poor photo of it. I'll send you a photostat. It is a glass house."

An image came to Arla of her own house, seen from a higher rise. In the image, her house was glass and she was able to see through the house, wall to wall. "How big is the house?" Arla asked.

"Not so terribly large. I don't have the exact dimensions. But they refuse to let it leave their hands. You must persuade them to let us have the house for the show. We would want it on loan for a minimum of six months."

"How do I persuade them?"

"That is up to you, Arla. But we must have it. It is the most imaginative American piece."

"I'll try. But if they never lend it . . ."

"No. Well, there is a first time."

By lunchtime the day was less sunny. Like a person who is too happy, it peaked by noon and the sky became a pale shade of gray. Arla drove through town out to the strip. Three years before, there had been two fast-food places; now there were five. The old shopping center had empty stores, but the big chains continued to buy contiguous plots of land. Arla wondered if the land around her house would ever be developed. It sat safely in the middle of nowhere, but so had the hamburger stand she pulled up to now. If it were ever developed, she would have to leave. When she thought this, the glass image came to her again: house, walls, all transparent. She ordered giant cheeseburgers with the works for herself and Bob, then waited outside for the food. In the east, the sky was trying to clear. The smell of grease from the open window of the hamburger stand made her feel sick. When she got into her car carrying her package of food, Arla found she couldn't breathe deeply. Her heart was beating hard. It couldn't be the cheeseburgers yet, she thought. She put the package on the seat next to her and rolled down her window. She put her head on the steering wheel. She felt so sad, as if she'd lost something and couldn't remember what. She had no reason to be sad. Nothing was happening. She felt a thick nostalgia— perhaps for spring, she thought—and she tried to take in the damp muddy air.

Joseph's Volvo was in the museum parking lot when Arla returned, and she could see him and another man by the site of the glass wing. They were moving around, talking and pointing. She entered the museum by the front door, left her coat in the cloakroom, and walked through the galleries looking for Bob.

"You're tracking mud," he said.

"It's mud season."

"Mies van der Rohe is here."

"So I saw."

They talked about gardens while they ate their cheeseburgers. Bob always put in three tomato plants and one row of lettuce and left it at that. Arla was trying to persuade him to help her rototill her garden in exchange for squash and cucumbers when Joseph came to the door of her office. He knocked softly against the doorjamb. She had listened for him so hard she hadn't heard his footsteps. "Hi," he said. "I was going to take you to lunch."

"Too late," Arla said. "Do you want the rest of this giant cheeseburger?"

"No thanks. How about dinner?"

"O.K."

"How about dinner at your house? If you still want to do that."

"O.K."

"I have to go to Troy to talk to the steel people, but I'll be back by closing time."

"Fine," Arla said, and Joseph nodded good-bye to her and Bob, then left. After they finished their cheeseburgers, Bob agreed to help her with her garden, but no sooner than the traditional planting day, Memorial Day. "Never give a sucker an even break," he said.

"Who's the sucker?" asked Arla.

By the time Joseph and Arla drove in caravan to her house, the sun was nearly finished setting. The light was soft. Arla parked her car in the garage and watched as Joseph parked his car, got out, reached inside for his jacket, and slammed the door. "Lovely country," he said.

"This is the worst time of year for looking at anything," she said.

"It's a great collection of barns. I like the way the buildings are sited."

"There was another one here originally—a big horse barn—but one of the past owners had it torn down. He sold the timbers and siding to some contractor."

"I loathe barnboard indoors," Joseph said. "The only thing I hate more than barnboard indoors is barnboard that's been sanded down and varnished and then put up indoors."

"It's very popular now. Let me show you around the outside while there's still some light. Then we can go inside and start dinner." But she remained standing where she was, looking at the place the horse barn had stood. On that Thanksgiving visit, her mother had said: "Arla. Go outside to see where the horses lived. You see what you'd like to do with that barn." And the teenage Arla turned angry and went outside. Her mother thought she was a child who would like to play in barns. Her mother had missed her growing, she thought, probably too sick and tired to take in the change. She hadn't gone into the barn, but stood as she stood now in the almost cold air. When she found the house again, the barn was gone. "Here," she said to Joseph. "Are those good shoes, do you mind walking around?"

"These are L. L. Bean mud shoes. Please."

They walked around the house and Arla pointed out repair work she'd had done on the foundation, the new roof and the new window over the kitchen sink. "I think it looks like a beach house sometimes," she said. "The window's so different from the original ones. It's from a Victorian house, so it's from a period sixty years later at least."

"It looks fine," Joseph said. "If the Victorians had put in the window, you wouldn't have thought twice about it. This is a vernacular house; it was meant to have things done to it by whoever lived here, and it probably has all along. That's what's good about wooden houses. They can be changed easily. Do you know who else lived here?"

They were standing in front of the west side of the house, the setting sun hanging in the kitchen window.

"No," Arla said. "I didn't know any of the owners."

She showed him her vegetable garden, now a fence surrounding lumps of hay and weeds, dead plants disintegrating after the months of frost. She showed him the inside of the big barn and the good view east from the hayloft. As the last of the light disappeared, they sat for a moment on a hay wagon that had been abandoned near an apple tree, moved only when

Arla mowed the lawn. Joseph looked around and said, "It's a perfect kind of place. You can see all your land at once, which is all anyone deserves. The house is fine. It sits fine." The view from the wagon led down a long slope, down miles into the Hoosick Valley. Arla wished the sun would leave more quickly. She was cold and impatient to show Joseph more inside the house. "This is a place to keep," Joseph said. "This place is forever."

"I hope so," Arla said. "It's taking forever to do what I want with it." His presence was reminding her that when she first came to the house, she imagined that a man would come along who would fix everything. Each time she was faced with a bird in the chimney, a broken windowpane, she looked around to see if he'd arrived. She had given up, of course, and hired people, learned to do what she could for herself. She tried to keep the gardens simple: lawns, perennial beds along the stone wall to the south of the house, vegetable garden, one perennial bed along the road. Even those gardens were more than she could handle at the height of summer, and she welcomed the first frost. The man who would fix everything remained an image in her mind, and he returned to her in gardens. She imagined his strong back and his patience as he expanded the perennial bed and moved the sweet woodruff to the stone wall where it should have been all along. She looked down now into the fields along the road that waited to be cleared of old limbs and brush, apple trees waiting to be pruned; and thought of the unfinished upstairs, the barn waiting for a new roof.

"How can you stand it?" Joseph asked.

"Forever?"

"No," he said, "I have my own ideas on forever. I mean the quiet. I would go nuts here."

She looked away from him to the hills, then back to the house as if it too would hurt her; but she knew the house only made her vulnerable to hurt. "I like the quiet," she said. "That's why I moved here. Come inside and I'll make you a drink. Then dinner."

In the kitchen, she liked him again and for the first time became aware that he was tall. In the museum and the restaurant, she had focused on his voice, his hands, his eyes. He was six feet tall, he said, and the ceilings in the house only seven and a half. She didn't know why she should care that he didn't like the quiet. In her kitchen, he became a guest and she handed him a glass of Scotch with ice, motioned for him to sit at the table. There was a letter from her father in the pile of mail she'd picked up on the way home. She decided to read it when Joseph left, and when she saw beyond the meal to his leaving she felt courteous toward him.

"I'm supposed to find a glass house for Monique," she told him. "She called this morning. She wants it for the glass show. It's been in Vermont forever, and I'm supposed to get it somehow and bring it back to the museum. She was very serious about it. She made it sound as if I should kidnap the house if the owners won't lend it to us."

"Is it a large glass house?"

"A doll's house, I guess. Monique didn't know. I assume it's the size of a doll's house, only it's glass."

"I wonder if it's a felony to kidnap a house, or if it's simple theft."

"It doesn't sound as if kidnapping a glass house would be simple," Arla said. "But I'll do anything for the museum."

Joseph opened the bottle of wine he'd brought from Troy, and Arla took her pasta machine from the back of the cabinet. "We can make pasta," she said. "I've only made it once, but I guess if you can make buildings, you can make pasta." She mixed the flour and eggs with her fingers while Joseph set up the machine, screwing it onto the kitchen table, protecting the oak with a folded towel. "I made the sauce last summer," she said, and pointed to one shelf that held what remained of her crop of tomatoes, twelve pint jars of sauce. "I'll have to make more next year."

"You're really into this whole country thing," Joseph said. "The house. The garden. Canning."

"I guess I am. I take it you aren't."

"I don't know," he said. "Life is short. You know, a lot of architecture is about nostalgia for places like this—housing developments with the houses set just far enough apart for people to think they're on their country estate. Personally, I like to see people going by. I like cities. And there isn't exactly a lot of work for architects in New England."

"Except that here you are. Doing your best commission of the year. Isn't that a big deal, a wing on a museum?"

"It's a big enough deal. Monique had a rotten experience with one of the fancier architects on her Nantucket house, and when she saw pictures of a conversion I'd done in Providence, she thought she'd try me out. We've gotten along well enough so far."

"I thought you met her in California."

"She read the architecture magazine with the article on the Providence place in the plane going West. It was the 'synchronicity' that got her."

"How California," Arla said. "I never heard her use such a word."

"And then it capped it that I was from Galveston. More synchronicity. Galveston's been dying since the hurricane of 1900, and people just love that. The palm trees lining Broadway, the old mansions, the port—Monique had just been there for the weekend, visiting some nice rice and cotton people." He smiled at Arla. "That's as opposed to nasty oil people in Houston."

"You seem so cool about the money. Do you worry about surviving?"

"I'm not on an unemployment line now, which is where some of the best people have been for a year or so." Joseph tapped a knife on the oak table, and the sound was like a short drumroll. "Reality's reality. A recession isn't a good time to be out on your own, but it's the time I've got. And there are strokes of luck—the Martins are exceptional clients so far. They have money. They both plan to be far away during construction. Cairo. Amsterdam. And I've been lucky, Arla. I always have something going."

"What kinds of jobs do you do?"

"Anything. Big. Small. Kitchens for friends. They cost the most—kitchens and bathrooms. I'm getting a reputation for dramatic showers on Martha's Vineyard. Have you had much help on this place?"

"I've had advice on details from the people who've done the work, but no real design help." She waited for Joseph's comment. Arla worried that someone would come walking into her house and laugh at it, or say: those windows are in the wrong wall. She feared mostly that she would believe the stranger.

"You've done admirably," Joseph said. "Even given a limited budget, you've done admirably."

"Thank you. Well, I hope I've done admirably on this dough. It seems kneaded enough. Help me push it through?"

"There's something sadistic about this machine," said Joseph. "I'm glad I'm not pasta dough."

Arla put too much flour on the noodles after they were cut, but Joseph told her it was the best pasta he'd ever eaten. "The best." They sat in the back room after dinner, near the wood stove. They pulled the big maple rocking chair and the red armchair near the stove, though the night was almost warm and the fire had gone out long before. "I've thought about changing the furniture in this room," Arla said. "Just giving up and crowding everything around the stove. I didn't realize how close you want to be to it in the winter."

"Wait for summer," Joseph said. "You may move everything around again. You may move it every season."

"I suppose you could," Arla said. "I think of rooms as fixed. That's why you have a home, so you know where everything is."

"That way you don't bump into things in the dark," Joseph said. "That's certainly one of the things a home can be, but it doesn't have to be like that or anything else. It's just space, you know. I don't own much furniture. Nothing to bump into."

"I wonder how that glass house has survived all these years," she said. "I wonder how any glass survives. I break dozens of glasses a year in this house myself."

"I can see you're meant to work in a museum. Especially a museum with a famous collection of glass."

"I'm careful with the objects," Arla said. "At first I was reverential. But then, keeping inventory, the things become like sacks of potatoes. Monique owns so much. What you see is the top layer of the top layer. Not that I've broken anything yet. Some things just break. Did you know that glass can shatter if there's a flaw in it? Even if you aren't putting any particular stress on it. Just washing a glass, for example."

"That's not likely. Or common," Joseph said. "It takes real stress. It's nothing to stop doing dishes for."

"No, I wasn't thinking of that."

"I've been reading about glass, too," he said. "With the right glass for the right job, it doesn't break. And the wing won't be a greenhouse or a steam room."

"I'm sorry I said that on the phone," Arla said. "I'm sure it will be beautiful. All that light, as Monique says."

"Wait until you see the drawings," he said. "You may think it's beautiful or not. I think I got it right."

It was time for him to leave, dinner over, dishes washed. Arla stood at the sink and watched him stub out his thin cigar. She moved past him to her bedroom, where she'd put his coat, and through the window saw that the night was clear, black sky, white snow. He stood at the bedroom door and accepted his coat, stood looking down at her. It had been so long, she felt, since anyone had looked at her. Mornings, she put on rouge and lip gloss, more as protection against the cold than to help her looks. And at night she brushed her hair, put on a flannel nightgown, and went to sleep under heavy covers, feeling like *Little Women*. She wondered if Joseph reached for her, touched her, if she would feel it at all. She wore so many layers—tonight a sweater, shirt, and down vest—how could anyone touch her through them?

"Thank you," he said. "This was the nicest evening I've spent in a long time. In one of the nicest houses."

"I'm glad you could come," Arla said. "I thought you never

would. I mean, I thought you'd just want to eat in restaurants forever."

She moved past him to walk him to the door, and he followed through to the back room. At the door, he put his hand on the knob, then hesitated and turned back to Arla. He touched the back of her neck, then her hair, and kissed her, saying, "How would you feel if I stayed the night?"

Fine, she wanted to answer, fine, but asked herself if he meant stay with her or just avoid the drive to the motel. She felt, first of anything, a tightness in her stomach, worried that once her layers were off, he wouldn't want her body, if that's what he meant to have. But she said, "Fine. Yes. I'd like that," and held her face up for another kiss. Joseph put his coat on the rocker, and the chair moved backward and forward as they kissed. He smiled and looked so happy for a moment, Arla felt she'd given him something she didn't know she possessed. They stood there for a while, embracing as if they were old friends kept apart for too long, and then moved into the bedroom, turning out lights as they went.

He was a slow lover, touching as if he were memorizing, as if he would be able to draw her afterward. She didn't like it at first, felt they should be moving in a utilitarian way, and then gave that up, gave herself up to Joseph. He was so much larger than she that she rocked and moved with him as if she were a baby. He could make her do anything, could hold her high or turn her. He had a surprisingly tight body, hidden beneath the bulk of his winter clothing. There was something of childhood in his smell of cotton shirts and summer days. They made love once, "from necessity," Joseph said, and then again. Arla kept thinking that next time she would be more relaxed and next time she would be there completely, no thoughts of him not liking her. As it was, she was lost in Joseph for moments at a time, in touching him and feeling him around her. When he came for the second time, Joseph had her hands behind her head as if he were a holdup man, and Arla watched him. "God," he said. "Arla." Where was Joseph at that moment? He opened his eyes, returned to her, and loosened his grip on her hands, then kissed her. They held each other and talked about nothing in the dark; then they fell asleep.

Arla woke with a voice shouting to her, but when she looked around in the dark there was no more sound. Joseph slept on his back, his right arm over his heart. There was sincerity in his position, and the look of someone free from care. He must trust her, she thought, to sleep like that, exposed to any blow. Though she tried, Arla couldn't find the right position in bed or the right proportion of warmth and air to lull her back to sleep. She listened to Joseph breathing and thought that dawn wouldn't come for hours. She got out of bed and found her robe in the dark. Arla left the bedroom, closing the door slowly and quietly. Once she had closed the door, she wanted to turn back to be with Joseph again, but she'd left him as surely as if she had gone miles away. The hours before when they were together, the moments of listening to him sleep, were as far away as the playground swings of her childhood, as irretrievable. She went into the dark kitchen and stood looking out to the lawn and the hay wagon, barely lit by a dim moon. Why had she thought of a next time as they made love? One night doesn't mean another. Now he would be around the museum every day. If things didn't work out in some way between them, it could become difficult.

She saw the letter from her father where she'd left it earlier that night, and she opened the envelope. He wrote describing the weather in the city and Arla's stepmother's weekly routine: she did this, she did that, she visited an old friend of thirty-five years who was dying of cancer. He never mentioned Arla's mother directly, no recollections shared, but he wrote that the disease was not so violent as it is when it takes younger people. Arla tried to detect sadness in her father's letter, an echo of her mother's death, but there was none. Her mother had died at the beginning of spring, in April, and this season was for Arla the beginning of the end of her mother's death. Her mother went to the hospital for the last operation, returned home, then back to the hospital to die. Arla had no idea if her mother thought of anything beyond death, if she

looked up to the sky above Fifth Avenue and asked for re-
lease. They hadn't spoken of death, so she never said good-
bye or gave a salute to her dying parent. Arla stayed at school
and translated Vergil. She called the hospital every day. Easter, she stayed in the guest room at her father and stepmother's apartment so that she could visit her mother in the
hospital. Rather than take the Ninety-sixth Street crosstown,
Arla walked across the park, sometimes walking down to
Eighty-sixth and across to meet the Metropolitan, then daw-
dling up to Mt. Sinai. There were things she wanted to tell her
mother but didn't: how each piece of food in her father and
stepmother's refrigerator was labeled for a meal; how Arla
never finished any packaged food for fear she was taking too
much or depriving the milk, eggs, or English muffins of their
future. She put things back where she'd found them, careful
as a hotel thief. But she didn't want to bother her mother, and
Arla told her nothing.

The visits to the hospital weren't successful. Arla and her
mother had always done things together and had the daily
matters of life to discuss. Now there was nothing to say, no
conversation to make; so Arla sat with her mother for what
she thought was a fair share of time and then escaped. Once
her mother had reached out to hold her, and she had smelled
like another person, a hospital person, not her old smell of
strong soap and clean cotton and a womanly smell Arla
couldn't define. Her flesh was different, too, thin on bones
never noticed before, never before so exposed to view. Arla
regretted that her mother had died in the hospital, as if it
would make a difference now if her mother had died in her
house or another place. Her mother deserved a better place,
Arla thought, something to look at besides a reproduction of
Rouault's clown. People should be allowed to die in museums,
she thought. Her mother might have liked to die meditating
on the problems of a glass house, how to make a glass bed and
lie in it. Arla thought of turning on the kitchen light and making herself some hot milk, but instead she returned to the bedroom and Joseph. He stirred when she got into bed, and turned

away. She turned away from him also and was able then to
go to sleep once more.

Joseph left for Boston on Friday, saying he had an afternoon appointment. That day Arla wrote to Mr. and Mrs.
Peter Unterecker in Montpelier, Vermont, describing the museum and its collection. She told about the donation of the De
Nuys collection to the museum and the construction of the
new wing, planned for opening by Christmas. She asked them
to lend their glass house for six months. If she didn't get an
answer in two weeks, she decided, she would write again. If
that failed, she would telephone. Now she would be able to
report to Monique that she was trying to get the glass house.
When they consented, she would go to Montpelier with Bob.
They would bring a crate filled with Styrofoam fragments or
a crate built to the specifications the Untereckers would provide for the glass house. All the glass would come in such
crates—rough-cut lumber on the outside, velvet and shock-
absorbent padding inside. Other shows had been similarly
fragile and nothing had broken. The glass house would be
fine. She finished typing the letter, sealed it in its envelope,
and mailed it that day when she went to lunch.

The museum was closed on Monday, and Bob and Arla
took advantage of this to remove everything from the east
side of the building—exhibition cases, objects, benches, and
the show of landscapes. They were sorting out which objects
were to remain on display and which should be put into storage when Joseph returned from Boston. He had been gone
only a few days, but Arla thought he looked different—thin-
ner and tired.

"Hard weekend?" she asked.

"I slept," Joseph said. "I don't know if you'd call that hard
or not. I'm mainly going to be on the phone today with contractors and going over specs. Let me help you."

With three people working, the space was cleared quickly,
and Bob started shelving and storing the extra objects. Arla

was ready to return to her desk to type up the list of what was being stored, when Joseph asked her if she would like to see the drawings for the new wing. She was pleased and felt he was giving her something personal. Together they unrolled the large drawings on the table in the storage area.

"What I wanted," Joseph said, "was to stay with the classical spirit of this building. I didn't want to simply build an addition in glass. I think this design stays within the classical mode. But it isn't pretending to be something it's not." He showed her the floor plan for the new wing and then an elevation of the museum with the new wing. Under those two drawings were others. Arla concentrated hard on what he was saying about the new wing and where it would sit. He pointed out the glass-enclosed entranceway that would lead from the old building into the single open space of the glass wing.

"In the end, Monique agreed on glass. No solid walls at all. So it will be space primarily for objects and sculpture. I've made the entrance such that anything that can fit into the museum can fit into this wing. I wanted some transition from the wooden structure to the glass. I also wanted the wing coming off at this angle instead of at a right angle. The other one will also. Same angle. Same relationship to the museum."

"What other one?"

"The other wing," he said. "The wing for the new curator's office. Monique wanted three offices." He rolled up the drawings of the glass wing and showed the elevation for a wing coming from the west side of the building. It was placed symmetrical with the original wings, similar to the glass wing in shape, but with less glass and more wood. The plan showed three rooms and a reception space; two of the rooms were large, the third was smaller and taken up by built-in files. The large rooms held a desk and either a sofa-chair arrangement or a trio of comfortable chairs around a table.

"Who are those three offices for?" Arla asked.

"Director—that's Monique. Registrar—that's you"—pointing to the file room—"and the curator's office."

"It looks like I have less space than I have now."

"It's better organized," Joseph said. "So it won't feel small."

"Did she tell you to make my space smaller?"

"Of course not. But you don't need a reception area the way a curator does. And when she isn't there, you could use her office if you needed to."

"Who does a curator receive?"

"Other curators. Dealers. Collectors. Don't look so put-out."

"I'm afraid that's just what I will be."

Would she be there, or would they replace her with someone else, someone who would expect less, a recent graduate from college, the wife of a professor from a college nearby. She wondered if she would stand in the glass wing, work in the little office. She concentrated on Joseph's description of the drawings, the indications of doors and windows and the outside finish-work, as if imagining the place correctly would guarantee her safe passage there.

Joseph came home with Arla that night, and he stayed with her every night until he returned to Boston for the weekend. He never left anything behind, and each morning packed up his clean shirt, which he carried on a hanger, his kit bag with razor and toothbrush, and went out to his own car, as if he would never return. Arla decided not to comment on this—if he wanted to live in a hotel, maybe he treated every place like a hotel.

One night they stopped at the A&P for food. Sharing the choices, picking the brands, pleased Arla, and she was interested in whether Joseph would tolerate frozen foods, which she wouldn't, or whether he cared for the gold-, red-, or black-packaged A&P coffee. Yet he seemed oblivious of the domesticity and shared the bill with her as easily as if they were fellow accountants at a convention.

One night he took her to an inn in Vermont, just over the border, that had opened for the ski business. It was a Greek Revival building, same vintage as the museum, but in place of Monique's stark walls and wood floors, the owners of the inn had chosen pale colors on the woodwork, period wallpaper on the walls. There were Oriental carpets on the floor, scattered on the broad-boarded oiled pine floor. The dinner was just right, Arla thought, the wine enough to remind her of summer, the vegetables fresh, the arrangement of the food on the plate pleasing. She got a little drunk, she thought afterward, and perhaps she was looking at Joseph a little too openly. They were the only people in the smaller dining room. An older couple occupied the large dining room. Yet at each table candles burned. Everything was perfect, though in memory the evening was tainted. They got into the car and Joseph thanked her for her hospitality in the last week and gestured toward the restaurant as if to say taking her to dinner was the least he could do.

On the way home, they discussed the wing and the stages in which construction would occur: the excavation, he explained, would last until the end of the week; footings and the slab would be poured, scheduled for the following week, the first week in May. The steel was being fabricated, the glass had been ordered to size. Once the steel frame was erected, the glass would be delivered and installed. The finish-work was minimal: wiring, the floor laid for the storage space in the basement of the glass wing, a more formal floor for the exhibition space. "Monique wanted slate," he said, "but she's settling for carpeting. It'll hold the heat and soften the severity of the glass walls."

"Will the exhibition cases be glass or Plexiglas?"

"Plexiglas. Everything. Less fragile. Though glass for construction is hardly fragile. Despite what you think." He gave her figures for the stress factors involved, and the numbers reminded her of fat doughnuts dropped into his talk.

The backhoe that arrived on Tuesday to dig the hole was like a giant version of a child's tin beach toy. It had avoided ruining most of the front lawn and had maneuvered its way to the site without touching a tree. Where it crossed the lawn, it had ripped it up completely. She would have hated the machine if Joseph hadn't been responsible for its noise and earth-eating. As it was, she felt almost proud of it, as if it were an extension of Joseph.

Once they left the museum and started the ride home, they rarely talked about their work. They talked about the past—places they'd been, trips they'd taken as children. He'd traveled far more extensively than she, around the Southeast, the oil-producing states, with his mother and father. Still, in her car or his, they talked about cars, and the sense that as distance was eaten, time was eaten as well. He said he never felt so free as when he was starting out on a long journey, and she thought to herself that she never really felt free at all, or if she did, she'd never noticed.

Their time in bed was separate even from time in the car. It was as if the whole day was leading only to that nakedness, to being held and touched, with no idea of getting anywhere else, even to sleep. Sometimes during the day Arla wanted to tell Joseph about his nighttime self, as if he were two people, but she never did. She thought that in some way she must be missing some knowledge other people had about sex or love, and revealing her ignorance might cut her off from this nighttime source.

Arla thought of asking him if Monique planned to keep her on when there was a curator for the glass. An office for a registrar didn't mean that she was the registrar Monique had in mind. The digging over, the machine was quiet by noon on Friday, on schedule, its neck arrested in a startled position. The workers left and then Joseph did also. Arla came up to him in the storage space as he was packing his briefcase.

"Hi, there," he said. "I was going to come in and say goodbye."

"How do you like the hole?" she asked.

"They never look great," he said, "but this stage doesn't last very long. I'll probably be back by Monday. Tuesday at the latest."

"Why don't you stay here for the weekend?"

"I can't. I have things to do in Boston."

She walked him to the car, and he touched her arm in a sign of farewell. "See you soon," he said. "It's been a nice week, hasn't it?"

"Very nice," said Arla, and she watched Joseph's car go down the driveway and mix with the traffic leading away from the museum.

Crocuses were out on the lawn and there were buds among the green narcissus stalks. Arla remembered: spring came slowly and took hold fast. Before she could see what was happening, everything would be out—maple leaves, lilacs, apple blossoms, tulips—and it would be too late to put certain things in the garden. It rained that weekend, washing away the snow, even the high banks made by a winter of plowing. The rain made it impossible to do anything outdoors, and so Arla took everything out of the bathroom cabinets—towels, sheets, bottles, jars, old clothes and handbags, shoes and work clothes—and spread it over the kitchen to see what she would keep and what she would give away. She thought of going upstairs to sort out the cartons of discarded clothing and miscellaneous goods, but didn't. Instead, she read, listened to the rain, and sat in her red armchair looking out the window. She was waiting to get sick of Joseph Bird, but she hadn't yet. She saw him morning, noon, and night, and didn't seem to mind it. There was a neutrality to him that made this possible. Perhaps that was it; a distance that made her feel uncrowded by him even in tight spaces. She wondered if she would ever be happy with him, comfortable in her house or in his still-unseen apartment in Boston. He was smooth as marble, and when she tried to imagine suggesting to Joseph that she thought they could have a whole life together, she saw him unmoved and silent, polite and unreceptive. It would happen without speaking, or it wouldn't happen at all. She thought of him steadily, thoughts of him with her whatever she did; not so much thoughts or memories of things they'd done as the awareness of his presence in her, pressing on her. She took down her atlas at sunset on Saturday before she went out to dinner, and she tried to imagine Galveston. The map of Texas was no help. There were no hills, according to her map, but what did the flatness look like? Did it descend to the sea? The only sea she could imagine was the Atlantic at Montauk, seducing the dunes into itself. She wandered the house, looking for a sign that he'd been there, knowing he'd left nothing behind.

The rain stopped Sunday night, and on Monday morning the dirt roads were almost dry, reminding Arla there would be dust all summer. She drove past the Robo car wash and glanced its way. It looked more upright in the spring morning; what had seemed battered and fragile in the winter had survived another season. She thought of washing her car, then decided to let it stay the way it was. She didn't know how to start things, she didn't know how to let them continue. She wouldn't call it an affair with Joseph. If she were living in the city, there would be more sense of choice perhaps. She wondered if Joseph slept with her because she was there and if she had taken him for the same reason. No. She would want him in the city also, but still not have the words to carry her requests for reassurance and praise, for promises to think of her, to attempt to care into the future.

Midmorning, the truck arrived from Florida with the circus posters. Arla and Bob spent the morning uncrating the framed posters and setting them along the walls in the storage space. The truck driver drank coffee and watched them work. Arla checked the posters against the shipping roster and discovered that five more were listed than delivered. She spent an hour on the phone with the registrar in the Florida museum, who checked his copy of the roster and his correspondence with Monique and Arla. In the end they saw that Monique had arranged by phone for the missing five to stay in Florida and had never told Arla. The registrar had neglected to cross them off his list. Now, Arla realized, the two-page catalog for the show—already printed and stapled—would have to be reset or corrected with a new page. The mistake would reflect directly on the museum and Arla. At noon Arla signed the papers officially accepting delivery; then she and Bob stood on the portico, watching the truck leave. "I'll bet that driver was happy to get out of here," she said. "Why does Monique have to do something like that every time? This could have been simple."

"Well, it's over now. Isn't that Bird's car?"

They watched Joseph's car climb the drive, then Bob returned inside the museum. Arla walked over to Joseph in the parking lot. "How was it?" she asked.

"How was what?"

"How was Boston? Your weekend."

"It was all right," he said. "Let's go look at the hole."

The backhoe had left tracks in the mud, intersecting and mellowed by the rain until it was impossible to distinguish what had been there, what had caused the hole.

"It's rained," Joseph said. "The weather was perfect in Boston."

"It rained nearly all weekend."

"The concrete people come tomorrow. Footings and slab. This will look more like something then, less like a hole. Or a mistake." Still, he looked pleased by the excavation. Arla reached over and tried to take his hand, but Joseph moved away.

"Why?" she asked.

"For discretion."

"Who is there to be discreet for?" There were two visitors in the museum and Bob, no one in sight, no one to see them.

"First, for Leon and Monique. Then for ourselves," Joseph said.

"You've almost moved in," she said. "Practically."

"But I'm not really moved in," he said in a neutral tone, as if they were discussing the properties of glass or steel. "I have my motel room. My apartment in Boston."

"I know that," Arla said. She wished she hadn't reached for him or initiated the discussion.

"I don't want to impose on you," he said.

"You don't impose. I like your being here." She moved away a few feet, hoping the conversation would end. If she never brought up the subject again, perhaps they would grow closer together, and move on to the next stage of their relationship. She looked into the still-muddy excavation and saw him gone, herself without a job. "Maybe this is too fast," she added.

"Time goes on," Joseph said. "If you like it or not. If you think it's fast or slow. I'm only staying with you sometimes, you know."

"That's reasonable," she said, knowing she wanted more. She turned to look at him, and he moved closer to her, took her in his arms. She rested her head against his chest. He was so large and solid, a wall between herself and the rest of the day. "This isn't discreet," she said, and started to pull away.

"No," Joseph said. "But we don't have to carry discretion too far."

In the quiet before the concrete trucks arrived, Arla and Bob began to clean the glass on the circus posters. Each poster took a longer time than she would have thought—the wiping away of handprints and grease, and thick traces of unidentifiable substances. It was an activity that exemplified her job to Arla, for it would be noticed only if it were not done. Joseph was outside, waiting for the trucks. She could see him through the one window in the storage space. That morning, Joseph had called his old engineering professor in Troy and he'd told Arla he would be at her house late, after he'd had dinner with the professor and his family. He'd offered to stay at the motel that night, but she said no. He hadn't invited her to dinner and she hadn't asked to come. The phone rang and she went into her office to answer it.

"Arla? Monique here. I have fabulous news for us."

"Hello. What's the news from Amsterdam?"

"First. How does the building progress?"

"There's a big hole in the lawn. That's about all I can say. The trucks come today to pour the slab. Joseph said that will be finished by the end of the week. The steel and glass have been ordered. The steel comes the tenth of May. Week after next. So that's progress, Monique."

"The drawings are marvelous, aren't they?" said Monique. She sounded distracted.

"It's a good design," Arla said.

"I feel awful to leave you there in the museum during that mess."

Arla wondered why this particular mess made Monique feel awful, but she made an effort to respond. "It's so important, what you're doing there. Without your work, there wouldn't be any glass show at all. Really, I'm fine. I'm handling everything here."

"Yes. Of course. I have two very competent students helping me, you know. You'll meet them at the opening of the wing. I've thought about bringing them for the summer, to help you unpack. Label. That sort of thing. This collection is vast. It puts the museum on a whole new footing. Much more professional. I've gone to Paris. To the Rijksmuseum here. So different. Larger, of course. Listen, Arla, my real news is that I have finally found the person to write the catalog. He may agree also to be curator of the museum. We are discussing this very seriously. He's marvelous—Bernard von Saldern."

"He sounds German."

"He was a dear friend of my aunt and is a fine historian. A scholar. He knows glass. Definitely, and knows the collection as well. He has started the work already."

"Will he send the manuscript to me?" Arla asked. "The schedules make it so that we have to have the manuscript ready for the printer by the end of September."

"Bernard and I have discussed this thoroughly. He will send you the entries as he composes them. With the proper bibliography. Then you will edit them as they arrive."

"That sounds fine, Monique." She didn't mention that the bulk of her copy editing was best done when the manuscript was complete, or that she would be on vacation part of August. Amendments to Monique's plans were taken personally, and Arla tried to suggest changes by mail instead of over the telephone. "I'm sure it will work out. The circus show is here. The posters are terrific."

"I'm considering coming for a few days," Monique said. "Bernard wants to see the museum before he makes a final decision. Just for the weekend, Arla. No longer. There is too much to do here."

At the end of the day, Arla locked the museum and walked to her car. Bob had left early for a dentist appointment; Joseph was in Troy with his engineering teacher, and hers was the only car in the lot. She looked back at the museum and the mound of dirt from the excavation, at the piles of wood waiting to be made into forms for the concrete. She squinted to see the glass wing that wasn't yet built, to put the image from Joseph's drawings onto the site. The air was clear enough for her to do that, and for a moment Arla forgot everything and was absorbed in her vision. She saw the white museum, the lawn grown back as it had been before excavation. She saw the new glass wing with a sunset and a cloudy sky held in the glass walls. The walls were smooth. The polished panes of glass fit together as do the walls of a Japanese paper house or the pieces of a jigsaw puzzle. She saw the wing in February of a year she couldn't name, in the first light of day. Glass—glass was reflection and light, glass was liquid, and, for the eyes, glass would be warmth also, all the properties of air and fire combined. If Joseph had been there, she thought, she could have told him about glass.

On the way home, Arla saw a dead possum on the road. She was sure it was a possum. She had seen the gray fur and the pointed nose. And it wasn't playing, it was definitely dead. Or if not, she thought, she'd just seen the king of possums playing dead on the white line.

The house was quiet without Joseph. Sometime she would tell him about her mother and the house. She thought of going upstairs and starting to clean up, but instead made her supper and ate it at the kitchen window, looking out at the road. She would not rely on Joseph or include him in her future plans. He wouldn't help her with the house, she was sure. He might give her a stray afternoon, but he would keep his distance otherwise. That was all right. This way, if he left, he wouldn't take the house with him.

Arla went to bed early but couldn't sleep in the dark that was not yet complete and smelled of summer. She thought of whom she might have left off the invitation list for the circus show, of the new list of posters she had ordered, then got out of bed to make herself some warm milk and honey. She sat at the kitchen table looking at her hands; then she closed her eyes and listened to the sound of the flame against the pot, the wind through the trees, the refrigerator as it clicked off and left silence. Perhaps when people sat in a kitchen late at night, they wanted only this: to listen for nothing and to hear the ordinary sounds of the moment.

In the museum mail Wednesday morning, a letter came with the Untereckers' name and a rural-delivery address in East Montpelier crudely imprinted on the back of the envelope. Arla recognized the imprint from dollar stationery she'd ordered once from the back of a magazine. It was not the usual stationery of a collector or the owner of a rare piece. The letter, badly typed on a fading ribbon, told her they never loaned the glass house to anyone and they never moved it from its place in their house. "This house has survived," the letter read, "because it doesn't move." The letter was signed in green ink: "Charlene Unterecker." That sounded final enough, but it was only the first round. The acts of persuasion could begin. That morning Arla replied that she regretted their decision not to lend the piece but that she understood completely their concern for its safety. She mentioned a few other collectors who lent to the Martin Collection, saying that they and Monique herself lent only to certain museums under special conditions. At the same time, Arla assured them, their piece would be treated with the utmost care. The wing would, after all, hold the best private collection of glass in America, perhaps in the world. Great care was being taken to move the collection the great distance from the Netherlands to upstate

New York. The same care would be exercised in moving their glass house the hundred or so miles from Montpelier to the museum. Then she lied and wrote that she would be in Montpelier in a few weeks, at the end of May or the first week in June, for personal reasons. Would it be possible, she asked, for her to come and at least see the glass house, if only to satisfy her curiosity? She sealed the envelope and thought that wasn't a bad play. One foot in the door, Monique would approve. Arla wondered why she didn't leave them alone, but if Monique knew of the house, so did others. Monique wasn't the first and wouldn't be the last to try for the glass house. Still, Arla felt a certain reluctance as she mailed the letter to the Untereckers. Owning a glass house was bad enough. Being asked to lend it seemed the final blow.

Joseph was pleased with the progress of the wing. He had been correct—the foundation made it look as if there would be a building there, and fairly soon, he told her. "It's gone pretty much according to schedule so far," Joseph said on Thursday night. "The glass and steel shouldn't be any problem. The steel's promised for week after next. I'm going to Boston for the weekend, but I'll check back here next week. It's gone so smoothly so far. Most buildings have many more delays than this, even in a few weeks."

They sat at the kitchen table, Joseph smoking a small cigar, Arla holding a glass of wine in her hands.

"I wish this building was going as well as yours," she said. "I guess it all takes more time than you think."

"What's next in your plan?"

"The upstairs. This summer the carpenter is coming to do one of the upstairs bedrooms. I'll work with him for one week of my vacation, then paint the room the rest of the time."

"I've never been upstairs," Joseph said. "I think that's pretty amazing."

"I don't know how you were spared," Arla said. "Usually people get dragged up there first time in the house." She felt reluctant to take him upstairs or to go up herself, reluctant to be reminded of the work to come or of the postponed task of clearing away the boxes and suitcases.

"Let's go," Joseph said. "On your feet."

"Why now?"

"Why not?"

The stairs were genius, Joseph thought, fitted into half the space of a normal staircase, so that it was like climbing a boxed-in ladder. The floor beneath their feet was covered with a fine dusting of plaster and chunks of the stuff, though Arla had swept out twice. The walls were planks, cross sections of trees still marked where the plaster had been. "It's a mess," she said.

"It's perfect to be worked on—you'll save money on labor. It's easier to work in gutted spaces."

She showed him into the room she intended finishing that summer, a bedroom as large as the living room below it. It faced east over her neighbors' fields. The panes of window glass betrayed their age by imperfections; downstairs all the windows were new. Arla looked out through a double circle inlaid in the pane.

"I think there's a problem here," Joseph said.

He was standing by the south wall, his hand on the timber on which the rafters rested. Next to his hand was a flesh-toned growth as large as his palm. "It took a while for this to happen," he said, and pointed up to the exposed roof. The nails from the asphalt roofing material showed through at regular intervals; a stain ran from the pitch of the roof down to the timber. "This has been wet a long time."

"What do I do?" asked Arla.

"Fix the roof. I wouldn't be surprised if this weren't happening all over the roof. Sometimes this kind of thing doesn't get caught until it's too late. You're lucky, you know."

"How am I possibly lucky?"

"Think of what would have happened if you'd finished this room and the roof continued to leak. It would have been throwing away your money and labor."

"You mean I can't do this room?"

"You can," said Joseph. He walked out of the room, and she heard him in the other rooms, walking the perimeter of the upstairs, then returning to her by the growth. "There's a few more bad places," Joseph said. "It's hard to tell in this light. Maybe it could be repaired. Though I doubt it. I think it would be smarter in the long run to put on a new roof. Then put new materials into the house."

"In the long run we'll all be dead."

"Think of the years you'll have with a good roof before then. I'm sorry. But you are lucky, really."

Joseph left for the weekend on Friday, when the last of the concrete work was completed on schedule. He looked pleased with himself, Arla thought, as if it were his work one way or another that had made the wing go so smoothly. After Joseph left for Boston, Arla phoned the Norwegian carpenter and asked if he had time to come Saturday or Sunday to see about the roof. If there was a chance of getting away with it, she would have the roof repaired rather than replaced. He would come Sunday, he said, morning or afternoon.

Summer was on the way. Saturday morning Arla had a call from her friend Marilyn, who owned a house ten miles or so north of Arla's on the Battenkill River. They'd gone to college together and shared an apartment in New York until Marilyn married François, a photographer, who seemed to Arla the most ardent person she'd ever met. He'd run off to New Mexico with another old friend of Marilyn's and then returned. This visit upstate was the first time she'd seen them in almost a year. They were there to open their house for the summer.

They met at the only nearby restaurant, a redwood-and-glass building that overlooked a gorge and the next town. Arla answered Marilyn's questions—she was fine, she was still liking the country, the museum was doing well—and she did her imitation of Monique, about whom François and Marilyn always asked. "No, no," Arla said, in Monique's voice. "I think we'll just tear down the house. The mushrooms, you know. A bad business." Marilyn and François had had innumerable troubles with their house as well, and when Arla told about the growths and the leaky roof, Marilyn gave her the Latin name for the pale flesh-colored things. "We had to have the whole roof done, Arla," and she went on to describe the size of the hole the roof made in their budget, which was funny during dinner and less funny as Arla drove home alone. The night was almost warm enough to sit outside, but Arla hunched her sweater around her and stood in the middle of her yard. She looked straight up to the stars, then at the electric wire that ran from house to barn, and over to the roof. In the dark, everything looked like shadows and seemed unimportant. If it took another year to finish the upstairs, so be it, she thought. It was another summer now, visitors from the city, the garden, and all she could do was go along with it, just as if she'd chosen it all, down to the last detail of the rotting roof.

On Sunday the sky was very blue and pure-looking, the hard blue of the Norwegian carpenter's eyes. The roof was beyond repair, Ole said. Arla trusted him, and knew he would always rather repair than replace, and so she asked, "Will we be able to do the room upstairs even so?" still hoping he could pull the rabbit out of the hat.

"No," he said. "Funny thing. Comes to the same amount of money, but without a good roof the house isn't worth a damn. You're lucky you noticed it now. Before it does more harm."

When he left, Arla walked around the house, trying to see where the flaw lay in the roof, which shadow was a hole, but the roof was bland as ever, asphalt colored to look like slate. She went into the house and climbed the stairs, returning to the place on the south wall where Joseph had spotted the growth. At least she had the money to do the job; at least the repair was possible. Still, it seemed a bad omen. It seemed to tell her that she would never finish the house, that its completion would remain for her, as for her mother, always a little ahead, just out of reach.

Arla waited all day Monday for Joseph to show up or call her at the museum. She waited until 6:30 and then decided he wasn't coming and that she would go home. She took the long way home. She drove past two large farms that lay along the river and noticed that corn had been planted, was beginning to sprout. As she rounded a curve, the pale green lines in the fields widened into bands of color. Arla headed down a long hill to the flat river road, toward the Buskirk covered bridge. There were two boys fishing on the far bank beside the remains of a burned-out ice factory. Arla waved, and the smaller of the boys held up a string loaded with fish and shook it for her to see. The other boy just stared. She always wondered what she looked like to other people, but figured she would never know. On the other side of the bridge, the boys were hidden from her sight.

When she got out of her car, she heard her phone ringing and ran inside to answer it. Joseph said, "Something's come up. I have to stay another day or so."

"I'm sorry. What's up?"

"Some things haven't been going as smoothly as they might," he answered.

Outside the window, Arla's cats were parading slowly across the lawn toward the setting sun.

"Everything's blooming in Boston," Joseph said. "It's practically summer."

"You sound peculiar," Arla said. "Far away."

"I am far away. I have to hang up, Arla. I'll be back tomorrow or the next day."

They hadn't known each other very long, Arla thought when she hung up the telephone. Three weeks since he first stayed with her, and not everyone came as blank as she, waiting, having a house to fill. Joseph had someone in Boston. Maybe they were breaking it off or maybe they were deciding to give it another chance. A woodchuck came and stood on the lawn under the apple tree, staring at her garden. The sky was going black, and the lawn appeared very smooth and green.

The three cats struck poses along the stone fence, and Arla imagined a blue sky and a white beach, Joseph and a woman under the blue sky, giving it another chance.

"Where you been, lady," Clifford asked. They'd met on the road as she was hauling hay to throw on the garden. "We don't see much of you these days." He'd crossed the lawn without her noticing, and stood beside her, his hair combed, ready for supper.

"I hear your trucks going in and out," she said. "How's your family?"

"All well but for the mother-in-law." She was in a nursing home, and though Clifford had always been to Arla the kindest of neighbors, he had once told her he'd like to put away the old lady who no longer knew them from Adam. They talked about summer and their gardens; then Clifford looked away and started talking about the road. There was a letter from the highway department she hadn't opened. He explained that the town finally had gotten federal funds to pave the road below their houses and the dead-end extension up past the houses to Arla's barn. There had been two accidents that year around the blind curve and a section that washed out each spring. The road shook to death their neighbor's expensive tractors, and their own cars were being worn to a nub. But she and Clifford had always been against the paving —progress, they called it—and their neighbor, a serious farmer, wanted it. Arla and Clifford looked down her hill to his house and out past the road to his large fields. "They'll take down every one of these trees," Clifford said. "And that broken-down stone wall of yours."

"Can't they take down one or the other?" Arla asked.

"They can leave the whole blamed thing alone. You can stop them. You and me, fifty-fifty. But if it doesn't get paved, we don't get out next winter. If they can't use the big plows on this road, we wait until afternoon for the little plow. I can park my truck, and so can the boys down there, so we'll get

out. But you, lady, I don't know. You got to go to work every
day, unless you're planning on early retirement."

"But I get to work every day as it is. So far." Arla waited
for Clifford to say "Progress" and shake his head with her,
but he just repeated everything he'd said twice more, then
said, "Well," and went down the road. She watched until he
reached his house. He'd changed his mind. She would give in
because that's what Clifford wanted. The road would change.

Arla went inside her house, closed the door for the night.
She went to the back room, to the red armchair, to think it
over.

The lilies of the valley would go, and maybe the maple at
the corner of the lawn. Surely the maple would go, and if it
went, the oak would go as well. She would use them for fire-
wood, and three years hence, ash for the garden. The cycle
didn't displease her, but it didn't equal the sight of the full-
grown trees that guarded either side of the road. When she'd
bought the house, she hadn't banked on trees coming down
and flowerbeds being torn up. All her activities were in the
other direction, roots down deeper every year. Still, if she
could look ahead a month and see herself and Joseph settled,
the roadwork done or still undone, it wouldn't be intolerable.
But that was what was impossible—knowing about the building and tearing down.

She left her chair and walked around the house. Small
things were out of place. Plants needed water. Half-read books
lay on their stomachs. A cup of coffee, half-finished, sat next
to the telephone, and a rug was curled on the living-room
floor, kicked aside and never straightened. The sink was full
of dishes from meals before. Arla felt as if she were waking
up, seeing what was before her. Tomorrow, when she had the
energy, she would put the house in order. Spring was beginning. There was time for everything. And it would be stranger
for Joseph not to have unfinished business in Boston than for
him to stay there straightening it out.

After dinner, she felt well, a little high on wine and the

almost warm night air, the sound of moths batting against the window. She watched an old movie on TV and listened to the tree frogs singing in the background. Joan Crawford had a scar on half of her beautiful face and it led her to a life of crime. She met a plastic surgeon who straightened out her face, which changed her character. The movie depressed Arla. She thought it over as she was falling asleep—listening to the tree frogs, to the moths still faithful to the glass. Scars went deeper than that and stayed truer. It was a transformation too easy for Arla's taste.

Arla waited for Joseph to call the next day, and when he didn't, she assumed he wasn't coming back from Boston. There wasn't anything for Joseph to do on the wing for a week, and no reason for him to return. A potter whom Arla hadn't seen in a long time, a woman who threw perfect earthenware bowls and incised them with geometric designs, called Arla and invited her for dinner. Arla drove to the village where Lila lived in a converted chicken house, and they drank a little too much wine. She tried to describe Joseph to Lila, who was the only other woman she knew living alone in the country. Arla talked about Joseph only in the vaguest terms. Mostly, she said, it was so different to have someone around.

"I don't know," Lila said. "It's always like it is in summer around here. So great. Perfect. Then it's so painful when they leave, isn't it? And then all your soft feelings are like vapors. I never understand why I fell for someone once it's over. I think I'd rather just dig in for the duration, myself. In place of the sure thing."

When she reached her house that night, Arla couldn't remember one thing that had happened on the way. She'd driven almost blind. Joseph's car was parked in the yard. There were no lights on in the house. When she turned on the overhead kitchen lights, she saw signs of Joseph's presence—a bottle of Scotch and a tray of melting ice cubes, half-empty cardboard cartons leaking from the bottom onto the kitchen table.

Arla looked inside the cartons: Chinese foods, some kind of meat or black mushrooms, green vegetables in a thick yellow sauce. She walked into the bedroom and found Joseph on the bed. He was asleep. His shoes lay on the floor and he'd loosened his belt. He was on his back spread-eagled, taking up every inch of the bed, breathing heavily. When Arla got close to him, she could smell the city—Chinese food and Scotch. Joseph looked as if he were determined to sleep, and so she returned to the kitchen. She put the food from the cartons in bowls and put the bowls in the refrigerator. She washed out the saucepan Joseph had used to heat up his food, then got ready for bed.

Arla tried to climb over Joseph to get into bed, and he groaned a little. She thought she should have brought a glass of water with her in case he woke up later cotton-mouthed. It was hard to get under the covers with him taking up the bed. She tried moving him by rocking him gradually to one side, but he was deadweight. When she was ready to give up and sleep in the back room, he stirred and woke.

"Arla."

"You don't have to wake up. Just roll over so I can get into bed."

"I meant to be awake when you got back. I just went to sleep for a few minutes."

"That's all right."

He got out of bed and Arla went under the covers, trying to locate the warmth he'd left. She watched him undress, and was going to tell him what had happened that day at the museum, when she noticed four small Band-Aids on his abdomen.

"What are those for?" she asked.

"I went to a doctor," Joseph said. "He took off some bumps."

"What kind of bumps?"

"I'm surprised you didn't notice them. Just small growths. That's all."

"Why did he take them off if they were just small growths?"

"They rubbed against my clothing. They were getting irritated." Joseph went into the bathroom, and when he returned, the smell of toothpaste and soap had replaced the Chinese food and Scotch. He kissed her, then said, "Ready to fall asleep? I could go right back to sleep. I don't know what's wrong with me."

"Are you sure about those bumps? The doctor said he was sure?"

"That's what he said."

She wanted to make love or perhaps only to feel the closeness after lovemaking, but Joseph held her too hard for Arla to move or to turn. She tried to turn, but his arm was pressing on her neck, and so she gave up and tried to sleep as they were. It was dark in the bedroom, none of the usual shadows coming through the bamboo blinds. Her arm was falling asleep under his weight, and when Arla tried to move it, her hand brushed against the Band-Aids. Joseph's abdominal muscles contracted at her touch. "Sorry," she said. "Did that hurt?"

"No." She waited for him to say more, but he stopped speaking. She thought perhaps he had fallen asleep again, and then: "The whole thing was absolutely painless. The doctor just snipped them off and put these Band-Aids on." She could almost touch Joseph's desire to continue speaking. He didn't speak, didn't relax and sleep, but lay holding her and breathing as if he were measuring the air.

"Is everything all right?" she asked, and he didn't answer her. She wanted to talk and to hear Joseph talk. She wanted to bring them closer together. She wanted him to know her, though there was something satisfying in the way they lay absorbing the silence and the darkness. His arms around her felt massive and immovable. "I've never really told you about my family," she said. "It's funny, but we don't know much about each other."

He loosened his hold on her and turned onto his side, motioning her to do the same, so that they lay apart, facing each other. He took both her hands in his and held them together so that her wrists touched in a position of prayer. "Let's talk about your family, Arla."

"My mother died when I was in boarding school," she said. "I was almost sixteen."

"I think you told me that," he said.

Arla thought his hold on her wrists loosened, but she couldn't be sure. She stretched to touch his toes with hers, trying to warm him. "She died of cancer," she continued. "She lived in this house, Joseph. She used to own it. She never really lived here. She bought it for weekends and meant to live here sometime in the future, but she never got to do that. I didn't like it too much when she had the house."

"Did she leave you the house?" Joseph asked. "I thought you said you had a mortgage and all that."

"Her estate sold it. So that I could stay at school and go to college. But I found it again. Just by chance. And when it came on the market, I bought it."

"It's a nice house," Joseph said. "But why did you buy it?"

"Because I was happy here with my mother, I guess. She wanted to finish the house and never did. She didn't even get as far as I have."

"I've always liked the idea of cremation. So simple," Joseph said. "Just scatter and be done with it. You don't take up space anymore. I mean, everything should go with you when you die, so people aren't stuck with all your leftovers. You're a funny one, Arla. Buying this house."

"I guess," Arla said. "My mother didn't stick me with it. I wanted it."

He turned away and let go of her, and once he was asleep, Arla regretted that she'd spoken. She hadn't told him right. Before she spoke, she thought the words would come across with images that she wanted him to have—the house before she bought it, perhaps her mother sitting in the kitchen; and feelings—this feeling of return that was in the house. She'd said it all wrong. She hadn't wanted to own the house because she had been happy there with her mother, but because her mother had been there. So simple, as Joseph said. She hadn't told him in a way he could understand, and he hadn't understood a thing.

There was nothing for Joseph to do until the steel arrived in a week on the tenth of May, and so Arla went to work and he stayed in her house. In his absence at the museum, she began to look forward to the glass wing. She thought that being in it during a snowstorm would be like being inside a glass paperweight ball that held the landscape in a thick, clear liquid. When you shook the ball, she told Joseph, snow came up from the ground, then fell back down.

She went to work and left Joseph sleeping in her bed. When she returned, he was sleeping in another part of the house—Wednesday on the couch, on the lawn Thursday when the weather turned warm, in the back room Friday with the wood stove blasting heat. He had miscalculated the temperature, he told her. Joseph stayed awake part of the day. Arla saw signs of that when she returned from work. He mowed the lawn, all around the house and barns and down around the vegetable garden. He rebuilt the barbecue that consisted of bricks stacked in a half circle, corbeling the bricks and making the barbecue more secure; a Mesopotamian form, he said. He found the putty and her putty knife and reputtied the windows in the kitchen. "Paint them," Joseph recommended. "Or sooner or later they'll fall out." When she came home from work, she made them dinner, waking Joseph to eat it, talking with him during the meal, then washing the dishes while he fell asleep again. They didn't make love and she worried about his sleeping, but Arla thought that perhaps they had passed through a more sexual period and now were living a normal life together day to day.

On the weekend, Arla worked in the garden while Joseph slept in the morning; he took a long walk in the afternoon while she napped. He brought wildflowers back with him, squashed in his hand. On Sunday they drove to town together for the Sunday *Times*, then sat outside reading. Arla

was distracted by the breeze rattling the paper. The type
seemed too small to read outside, and after a while she lay
back, listening to the wind, listening to the hum of bees in
the maple blossoms.

"Don't you ever read the news?"

Joseph's voice came from a long way off—she had been
half-sleeping and at the same time was aware of the bees and
the sun.

"Don't you ever read the paper?" he repeated.

"I did read it. I read the art section and books and the magazine."

"Don't you think there's a world out there?" he asked.

"I listen to the news. I listen on the car radio as it happens.
Up-to-the-minute."

"I wonder if that would happen to me if I lived in the country," Joseph said.

Arla fell back into her half-sleep, thinking that was perhaps
the first time Joseph had shown curiosity about her habits.
She wondered if he was considering a move to the country,
but she chose not to ask, and tried, in fact, to forget it.

Around dusk, a car pulled up. It was Lila and a man Arla
had met once or twice before, a friend of Bob Walters', a
carpenter. They had come from a crafts fair in Albany, Lila
said, and were stopping for one for the rest of the road. Arla
took them through the house, giving them beer on the way,
and led them to where Joseph sat out back.

"I'm glad to meet you," Lila said, and Arla watched Lila
assess Joseph's looks. He appeared more hulking than when
they were alone, and more ordinary. The scene was domestic
—the ends of their lunch sandwiches, the empty glasses, the
crumpled sections of the Sunday papers.

"Looks like you've been having a better afternoon than we
have," the carpenter said. "It gets hot sitting around the city
selling your wares."

"Or not selling them," Lila said. "Three teapots. Four orders
for plates. One bowl. That was all right."

"City?" Joseph asked.

"Albany." The carpenter grinned. "That's the relative city around here."

It turned out that both the carpenter and Joseph knew a set of brick buildings in Albany that were "amazing." They started talking about beer, comparing Genesee and Lone Star for wateriness and nostalgic value. The carpenter had spent some time in Texas. So they talked about Amarillo and the plains. Lila and Arla watched the men talk, then withdrew into talk of their own—were the gardens in yet, had the weekend been good. Arla was pleased when Lila laughed at a mild joke Joseph made. The carpenter asked about the glass wing. He'd watched it being dug, he said, and had gone to the museum one evening to look at the shape of the excavation.

"The wing will be up soon," Joseph said. "The steel makes the biggest difference. Come by next week and I'll show you the drawings, if you like."

The offer seemed friendly, even excessively so, and Arla wondered if Joseph was counting on the carpenter not showing up. They finished their beers and Lila and the carpenter decided to leave. Arla and Joseph stood at the top of the road, watching, until they'd driven out of sight.

She lay in bed that night, careful not to touch him or wake him. Her skin was sunburned slightly, and she tried to put herself to sleep by thinking of the week ahead—the steel was coming, the invitations would go out—and of the year ahead. The wing would be well finished, perhaps the new offices also. Arla remembered the drawings of the office wing, the small room with files, the only office space for her. Unless she remained where she was. Joseph hadn't said anything about changing the present storage space. She might be allowed to stay there, even keep her files there. That could have been the true intention all along, and she hadn't asked Joseph the right questions. If she could talk to Monique about the plans, explain the importance of her job and continuing the work; but the importance was only to Arla, not to Monique. The museum, not Arla, was important to Monique, and as long as

someone did Arla's job, it didn't matter who it was. The curator for glass might be a new broom who would sweep Arla
clean.

Sometime near dawn, light just outlining the hills, the
phone rang. Arla didn't know how many times it rang before
she climbed over Joseph, then crossed the cold floor into the
living room to answer it.

"Arla? Monique here. I wanted to catch you before you
left for work."

"Would you hold on," Arla said, and put the phone down
while she got a blanket to wrap around herself. "All right,"
she said. "How are you?"

"I have made up my mind," Monique said. "In two weeks,
Arla. Monday the twenty-second. When I have the exact
times of arrival, I'll wire you. Bernard is coming as well. It
will be a good opportunity for him to see the museum, you
see, and he will help us hang the circus show."

By now Arla was fully awake, trying to think of something
to say to Monique. Monique was coming to the circus show.
For the first time in years, she wanted Monique to notice her
—her efficiency, her control of the museum. "So you decided
to come. Do you want the museum closed that whole week?
I was thinking of only closing for a day or two before the
opening."

"Of course, as usual, we will close the whole week before
a new show. There is no reason to change that."

"It's such a simple show to hang."

"There are details to everything, Arla. Have you ordered
the wine? The backgrounds are the colors we chose? Napkins.
You see, there are always things to think of, but of course you
do, Arla. Have you made arrangements for that glass house in
Montpelier?"

"Montpeelier," Arla corrected automatically. "They answered my letter about a week ago and refused to lend the
piece. So I wrote them another letter and told them the piece
would be cared for, nothing to worry about. I may go up there
sometime myself to speak with them."

"Bernard is eager for the piece. It isn't crucial—the collection is vast. But I want you to be sure you are doing everything you can. Go up by all means if you think it wise. Don't disturb them, though. They sound rather eccentric."

"I'll do my best," Arla said, wondering which was more eccentric—to wake people at dawn to tell them you'll arrive in two weeks, or to refuse to allow a fragile glass house to travel. "I'll keep you posted." She would have said more, but Monique severed the connection.

She returned to bed and wondered if she would be able to sleep again. She had the feeling that Joseph was awake—surely he had heard the phone as well as she—but he didn't move. She didn't have much hope for the glass house. The Untereckers would never lend it. Still, if she could secure the house for the show, it would convince Monique that she was indispensable. The thought pleased Arla. Nothing dramatic ever happened in the museum, but securing that piece would be drama. The glass house might somehow save her.

They decided to take two cars to work the day the steel was due to arrive. "I may want to stay later than you," Joseph said. Arla followed him to the museum and parked her car beside his. The day was clear as winter and cooler than it had been. Joseph looked awake and better than he had for a week. He was happy about the steel, she thought, and happy Monique was coming, as if showing Monique the wing would be more meaningful than showing it to her or Bob or any of the workers. And it would be, Arla thought. It was Monique's wing. In the parking lot, Joseph stood looking up at the museum and the wing. "I don't suppose it could have been better placed," he said. "Not without moving the museum."

"Did you think about doing that?" she asked.

"For at least ten minutes. It still could have been in a different place. The other wing may crowd the building."

He settled at his table in the storage space and Arla lost track of him for the rest of the morning. The wine had come after she'd left the night before, and she and Bob moved the

cases to a corner out of the way, under the raised arms of a
twelve-foot stuffed bear, a piece of sculpture Monique had
abandoned years before. The bear had cost only slightly more
than Arla's salary for a year, but she'd grown used to him,
even ended up feeling sorry for him. She called the Untereckers, but there was no answer. And in the morning's mail, the
first batch of entries for the glass catalog arrived from Bernard
von Saldern. She Xeroxed them and put the extra copy in a
file she made for them. As she was walking from the Xerox
machine to her office, she passed Joseph. He was on the phone
with someone and sounded annoyed. She noticed that he had
drawn nearly perfect circles over and over until the paper
split underneath his mechanical pencil. The steel was due any
minute; perhaps he was nervous about the walls going up and
enclosing the wing. Perhaps he really thought he'd put the
wing in the wrong place. She went back to her office and
began to look through the entries. The first object was a globe
within a globe. Von Saldern described it, gave the dimensions,
then noted that incised on the outer globe and decorated in
red and blue were the outlines of constellations and the signs
of the zodiac. A brass lever could be employed to turn one
globe and move it around the inner, stationary globe. For the
first time, Arla looked forward to seeing the glass show, and
she thought: If the crate were dropped, would the outer globe
break first, or the inner? She leafed through the other five
entries, then looked at the footnotes. There was something
wrong with them. Arla began tracing one book from entry to
entry. It was cited differently each time. Von Saldern included
a few decorative-arts books and a few journals that Arla
happened to know. In each case something was wrong—a
misspelling in an author's name or a title, the wrong publisher,
what looked like an incorrect date. No mistake was disastrous
in itself, but Arla knew how much time and energy each correction would take, how much research each small tedious
point required to be corrected and each correction justified to
von Saldern. Monique didn't care. They had been through
this before when Arla found mistakes in a catalog prepared

by a friend of Monique's for a show of Algerian rugs. The friend was a friend and a scholar, and Arla was Arla—Monique wanted her to fix it and be quiet about it. And so she would with the glass catalog, but the hundreds of entries and footnotes oppressed Arla. And in August, when she thought she would be making her house larger, making a new bedroom for winter, she would be mowing the lawn and watching the roof be repaired; no progress there.

Bob and Joseph came into her office, and Joseph asked, "Don't you listen to the weather report? Doesn't anyone pay any attention to information from the outside world?"

Arla looked out the window and saw the snow. The tenth of May, and the snow was falling thickly, gaily. "I listened to the weather report," Bob said. "Snow was predicted for northern Vermont and Quebec. They didn't mention anything about eastern New York."

"Will this make the steel late?" Arla asked.

"The steel's not coming," Joseph said. "They didn't even get the materials until last week. If they'd told me, I would have rearranged my schedule. Not waited around. Somehow the guy thought he could get done in three days what he'd planned for three weeks."

"Maybe he can," Arla said.

"No way. There's no time. It's just all so stupid."

When they left Arla alone in her office, she watched the snow coating the lawn and the cars, the foundation of the glass wing, and the apple blossoms. If it were snowing in northern Vermont, Mrs. Unterecker might be sitting in a parlor watching the snow through the walls of the glass house. Arla dialed the Untereckers' number in East Montpelier, let it ring twenty times, and hung up. She'd called so many times that week that she knew the number by heart.

Almost noon, Arla thought about going for lunch. When she went out in the storage area, she saw Joseph put down the phone and his pencil, then lay his head in his arms. He didn't turn as she came to him, and she stood still, watching, until

she realized he'd fallen asleep as quickly as that. He'd written
the name of the steel fabricator on a pad in standard architect's hand and the word "glass" below it in formal script.
He'd printed a phone number with a Boston area code and the
date of the coming Friday. Why was he asleep, Arla wondered, why did he sleep so much? His deep and sudden sleep
reminded her of the winter following her mother's death:
snowy afternoons, the sound of the teachers giving lessons in
American history and Latin, and Arla falling into a pit of
sleep.

She walked past Joseph and put on her jacket. Outside, she
brushed the wet snow off her car. Maybe Joseph was ill or
depressed, and that was why he slept, but the steel not being
delivered wasn't the worst thing that could have happened.
Joseph would see that in a while. Halfway down the drive,
Arla remembered that she'd left her wallet in the office. She
jerked the steering wheel and the car looped to one side then
spun down the drive. She took the steering wheel in both
hands and tried to turn the car left or right, but the car continued in circles down the wet drive. The trees, Arla thought,
I should stay away from the trees. She turned the wheel one
last time and the car went straight into a mound of dirt left
over from excavation. Arla sat still, looking ahead at the cars
going by on the highway. She backed the car off the drive,
turned off the engine, and got out of the car. She walked back
up the driveway to the museum and went into the storage
room.

Joseph's head was still down on the table. Her hands were
shaking and she felt like crying. Out the window, she could
see that the snow had already covered the spiral pattern her
car had made. Arla walked to the sink and unplugged the
percolator. She poured the morning's coffee and hot grounds
into the work sink. The fumes rose up and mixed with the
sink's smell of paint and soap. Joseph stirred and Arla turned
to him. He raised his head and looked around as if uncertain
of the time, of his location. He looked unhappy and puffy, and

Arla said, "Joseph," meaning to tell him she might have been killed. Instead she said, "Joseph. I'm glad you're awake now. Would you like some lunch?"

The next morning, the air was warm and fragrant. Listening to the news that the apple crop fifty miles south had been ruined by the snow, Arla felt sleepy and peaceful. Joseph was eating toast and talking about what he would do that day. "I might as well get in touch with the glass people," he said. "Once the steel's in place, the glass can be installed. And if everything goes right, it's a quick process." Arla wished they could take the day off from steel and glass, take a picnic in the woods. Then she heard Joseph say, ". . . and then it isn't necessary for me to be here except once a month. At most. I'll be back next week sometime, probably."

"Where are you going?"

"I just told you. Boston."

"Sorry," Arla said. "I was thinking of something else."

"There's nothing to do here, and I may be able to stir things up there. A cousin of Monique's has been talking about a house in L.A."

"Soon?" Arla asked.

"Sooner than later," Joseph said. "This is great raspberry jelly," he added, and smiled at her. "Nice morning."

Later that day, at work, she looked closely at the circus posters. Their glass was cleaned now, and they waited, like the wine, for Monique's arrival. She looked at the smiling heads of the clowns, the open mouths of the lions and tigers, the elephants balanced and erect. Here the circus was colorful and flat, here was the intention of the circus. But the circuses she remembered from childhood had scared her. There were too many things going on at once, too many sounds and too many smells, and she was never sure she was looking at the right things. Joseph had been annoyed about the steel because it meant he couldn't get away. Yet he'd sat at breakfast and told her his plans in an open way, not as if he would leave her just like that. He held her every night, tight so that she couldn't move, as if she were the one trying to get away.

That night after dinner, it was warm and Joseph and Arla wrapped themselves in blankets and sat outside watching the stars get brighter. Joseph talked about a vineyard he'd seen in California, its stubby pruned vines orderly as a housing project. "Haven't you ever wanted to travel?" he asked.

She wondered if he meant, would she travel with him, but she answered: "I've never been much of anywhere. I've traveled around the East Coast. One summer we went to Savannah. I'll travel when the house is finished."

She leaned back onto the ground and arched her head so that she could see the shape of the house against the sky. Other people's lives looked logical to her. She could see them in progression, one thing after another. Everything that happened to her was like one drop of rain after another.

"Have you ever thought about being dead?" Joseph asked.

"I think about it all the time," Arla answered. "Because of my mother."

"Your mother," Joseph said. "You told me about your mother."

"I don't think so much about being dead," Arla said. "Or even of dying so much as hearing the news. That's what I dread the most."

"Is it? That's a funny thing. That's only the very beginning of dying. It isn't even the real beginning, because by the time you hear, it's already taken place," Joseph said. "There's already been a certain progress to the disease. Whatever it is. We're dying from the moment we're born. Little children on their way to graves."

"Yes. But until you're told, it isn't real. It isn't official yet."

Before they went to sleep, she dialed the Untereckers' number. Ten at night, there was no answer. Arla and Joseph made love that night, and Arla forgot who Joseph was and if he were leaving or staying. When he fell asleep, he was holding her in the same tight hold, but when she tried to pull away he relaxed and let her go. She turned on her side and fell asleep. In the morning she woke before he did and remembered he

was going to Boston that day. His face looked peaceful, a
stranger's mask in sleep.

   She tried the Untereckers each day for the next week, dial-
ing their number three times—morning, afternoon, night—as
the time slipped away and the arrival of Monique and the new
curator came closer. Joseph didn't call and she didn't know
when he would return. The new date for steel delivery was the
nineteenth. She didn't call him, though she thought about it
while the phone rang endlessly at the Untereckers'. If she
asked, perhaps he would come with her to the Untereckers'
when she went to see the glass house. But she didn't ask, and
the best moments of the week were when she forgot about
Joseph and the glass house, forgot about the new curator and
Monique.
   On Wednesday, a week after the snowstorm, the day was
bright and warm. Arla stayed at work after Bob had closed up,
checking the invitation list to be sure there was no one else to
invite, writing a second confirmation letter to the circus school
to be sure they would come as they'd promised. She walked
through the museum, approving it as she did. She felt as comfortable in the museum as she had anywhere. It seemed impossible that Monique would fire her or that she would ever
work anywhere else. This was what she was good at, caring
for things, other people's things, keeping track, preserving,
cleaning, correcting. She did everything right. She did everything efficiently. Monique was capable of anything, but why
would she cut off her nose to spite her face and get rid of
Arla? She wouldn't ask for a raise this year, and the subject
wouldn't arise from Monique's side. When Arla closed her
eyes, she saw her own house and the museum, as if both places
were equally hers. She looked out the window at the new wing
as it waited for walls and glass. There was a chance it could
all work; she felt that today. Perhaps something could work
also with Joseph, but thinking of him, a heaviness returned.
Arla walked through the museum, closing doors, checking
lights and window locks, though Bob had done this an hour

or so before. The museum was quiet, ready to rest for the night. She closed the front door, turned on the alarm as she did every night, and went to her car. She sat for a few more minutes looking at the incomplete wing; then she drove home.

Going through town, Arla couldn't remember the inside of her house. She concentrated, but it had been cleared from her memory. Then she took the first turn past town, drove up the cemetery hill, and her memory returned. She played with the memory, blocking out the kitchen or thinking of it as it had been when she found the house again and when her mother had it. When she'd gone the last five miles, Arla was thinking so hard that at first she missed seeing what had happened that day. The old dirt road had been ripped apart by the passage of two giant machines now parked for the night in her front field. Three trees—two maples and an oak—were down. She parked the car and got out, walked back down the road to inspect the damage. In front of the house, the bed of lilies of the valley— still pips—had been ripped in half. Leaves and buds that would never bloom were ground into the dirt. Half of her perennial garden and a thick rosebush were pushed into a mound of dirt. The trees themselves lay with their roots sticking up in the air, torn and undignified. Though the house hadn't been touched, it looked as ruined to her as the road and the gardens. The house was exposed now to the road. It was no use saying things grew back. By the time new trees re-placed the old, she would be dead a hundred years. Arla walked to the house and sat on the front steps, looking at the road, waiting to cry, but she didn't feel much of anything but that first surprise that this place of all places had changed. She had let it go. She could have stopped it and she didn't. She forgot and was as careless as anyone, more careless per-haps. She would forget the way the road had been before, and she would probably accept the destruction. The only place the trees were alive now was in her mind, and it was not so good a place, it seemed to her.

She went into the house and down to the cellar. She opened the big freezer and stood before it. She stared at the packages of frozen meat, the cloudy plastic bags of vegetables from last year's garden, the containers of stock marked "CHK 10/76," "VEAL STK 9/76." She closed the freezer again. Upstairs, Arla poured herself a glass of milk and made a peanut-butter sandwich. She'd swallowed one bit before she saw that the bread had spots of blue mold. She couldn't remember if blue mold was good or bad, so she threw the sandwich away. The phone rang and it was Joseph, who said only, "Arla."

"Yes. It's me, Joseph." She looked out the window at the road damage. "They came and wrecked the road in front of the house today. I didn't know it would be like this. They ruined the garden out there and the lilies of the valley. All the trees down the road."

He didn't speak and she listened to the sound of air coming over the phone. "I don't mean to be unsympathetic," he said after a time.

"What do you mean?"

"I have some news that may throw this road thing into perspective."

"Are you going to California? Where are you now?"

"Do you know the car wash in town?" Joseph asked. "Robo?"

"Yes."

"Meet me there."

"Why can't you come here? I haven't eaten yet. Have you?"

"Just do as I ask. Meet me here, Arla."

The sun was setting as Arla drove past the last big farms before town. When she reached the car wash, the light was hitting the trees on the school lawn, making long black shadows across the green. Joseph's car was in one of the bays of the car wash, shining wet. She wondered what could be so important; it seemed that Joseph had told her everything he ever wanted to tell her. She parked her car by the vacuum and walked over to Joseph. He was standing with one hand against the wall of the car wash, and as she approached, Arla could hear him tapping lightly against the aluminum siding.

"Do you know what sound this makes?" he asked, tapping with his fingers.

"No," Arla said. "I've never stopped here before. I always pass by."

"Listen." Joseph tapped again, and they heard a sound which was without resonance. It was an ugly dull little sound. "The news is," he said, "I spoke to my doctor in Boston. I have cancer. Bowen's Disease. I didn't want to tell you about it in your house. For obvious reasons. I called the doctor last week and he wanted to see me. I went there and he confirmed the diagnosis. It's a form of the disease that will take about eight years to attack viscerally. Then it should be over quick enough."

"Eight years," she said. He would be forty then, not even forty. "Joseph. Why is it eight years?"

"Does that seem the wrong sum to you? Does it seem long? It doesn't seem like anything to me."

"Aren't you going to go to another doctor? How can you be sure this one is right?"

"I have been to another doctor. This is the second doctor. That's enough poking and cutting for me." His face didn't have much expression. His voice was even. She found herself looking at his shoes, as if they would help.

"What about chemotherapy?" she asked. "What about everything else?"

"There's nothing that can be done for years yet. And I may not do it even then. I may go back to Galveston. There's a medical center there." Joseph's voice had the same tone as when he spoke of the fabrication of glass and steel. He sounded reasonable, distant. Even then he had his odd confidence. She remembered the road then, the trees down, the gardens ruined. She put out her hand to the wall and leaned.

"Joseph," she said. "How do you feel?"

"I'm not in any pain," he said. "The doctors said there wouldn't be any discomfort for quite a while."

"But, Joseph. There are other doctors to see. There are

clinics that specialize in cancer. You have a long time to find some way."

"I believe this doctor. I believed the last one, too. I'm not interested in wasting what time I have. I thought you'd be suggesting things like that. And I wanted to tell you, Arla, I'm willing to face facts. I'm not interested in monkey glands and special clinics and doctors and going from place to place. I hate doctors. I hate being sick. I won't do it."

"What will you do?" she asked.

"Finish the wing. Go to California probably. I'll build a guesthouse on a cliff. That'll be appropriate."

"What do you mean, appropriate?"

"A little joke. I was thinking of the earthquakes they have in California."

"Then you won't stay here," Arla said. "You could, you know."

"I'll come back to see the building. To do the office wing, if Monique wants. At every stage, I'll check back."

"But, Joseph," she said. She wanted to ask: What about me? but there was no room for the question. It must have cost Joseph something even to tell her, to talk to her at all. The sun was low enough that the automatic spotlights came on in the car wash for the night, and Joseph and Arla were flooded with the harsh light. "Don't you want me to stay with you?" she asked.

"You can't leave here," Joseph said. "Between the museum and your house, what is there to leave for?"

"You. To come with you."

"No," Joseph said. "We wouldn't make it. There isn't anything in me for you."

"Nothing?"

"Not even what you think there is. I don't suppose you know me very well. Nor I you. I'm sorry, Arla."

"Why did this start? Why did you let it?"

"I didn't know any of this for sure. I hoped something else might happen. I can't think about this kind of thing now."

The tightening in Arla's throat grew worse, as if she were

the one who was ill. She tried to breathe but couldn't. She looked at Joseph, then turned and walked toward her car. Joseph followed her, and she got inside the car. Once she was there, the tears that had wanted to come receded. She was empty also, she thought. There was nothing in her, either.

"We can't stay in the car wash all night," said Arla.

"I'll see you tomorrow at the museum. When the steel arrives."

Since she was already in the car, her hands on the steering wheel, Arla didn't argue. And she wanted to get away. She looked out of the car at him and thought of the week before when they'd made love and she had been so glad she forgot who he was. She hadn't known him really for five minutes of their time together, and now he was proposing to leave her and die so far off in the future she might not remember him at all. She wondered why he had bothered to tell her at all, why he didn't just go.

"If that's the way you want it," she said. "If it's really what you want."

"I want to be alone tonight," Joseph said.

He would leave. She was no longer afraid. There was only a corner of hope in her, but she would get rid of that too. It didn't matter that he'd left clothes in her house or his toothbrush or a notepad. Those signs she had read incorrectly also. "Joseph," she said, "let's not leave it this way," but she said it so that she wouldn't reproach herself later with leaving it unsaid. What she wanted to do, she did, and so did Joseph. He said, "Good night. Good night, Arla," and she started up the engine. When she'd driven a quarter of a mile, she looked back through the rearview mirror and saw Joseph walking toward his car. When she'd driven through town, past the light and the big hotel, over the railroad tracks and past the turnoff for the hospital, Arla pulled off the road, sat for a few minutes, then reversed her direction. She retraced her path and drove as fast as she could back to the car wash. But by the time she got there, Joseph and his car were gone, no trace of them anywhere.

Arla woke with the feeling that something had gone wrong, and she remembered what it was. She looked around the bedroom as if the walls had something to add, closed her eyes, and tried to sleep again. Her sleep had been blank and unpopulated and she would welcome it again. She tried thinking of something far away—an image of the Pantheon came to her—but that looked like another museum. She was deciding to give up and get out of bed when the phone rang. It could be Joseph, she thought, though she knew it wouldn't be.

"Arla. Have I woken you?"

"No, Monique. I was just about up."

"I'm in New York with Bernard."

"I thought you weren't coming until Monday."

"No, I wasn't, but now I'm here. We plan to come up maybe tomorrow, perhaps not until Saturday. Bernard is eager to see the museum files and records. All that. He is so marvelously organized, Arla. He'll straighten us right out with true professional methods."

Arla thought that if his footnotes were any indication of his professional methods, he could pour chocolate sauce over the files and call it reorganization. "That's fine, Monique. I'll be ready."

Over coffee, Arla thought of the week ahead. Spending time with Monique always involved several phones ringing at once, preparing papers and calculations and then waiting, or watching the work rejected. Monique would find something wrong with everything—the color of the walls for the circus show, the kind of wine. And Joseph too would be dancing attendance on her, showing her the wing, explaining the next stages. And Joseph too would no doubt be making renovations and changes, doing hurried drawings and making changes for Monique, though he wouldn't change anything for Arla. She herself would stand there waiting to give, waiting to provide, and silent, as far back in the woodwork as she could recede.

She walked to the other side of the house and stood looking out her bedroom window where in winter she stood to watch the sunrise. The road men were arriving for work, climbing onto the machines in the field below. The road was smashed as it was the night before. The flowers scraped up by the machines were barely alive. She could save them if she dug them up now and transplanted them down at the stone wall along the lawn, if she watered them heavily that morning and night, if she protected them from too much sun, too much water, if she cut them back and waited a year to see if her efforts had succeeded.

She would put up with it all, she thought, with Monique and Joseph, with the road and the dead flowers. But she wouldn't lift a finger to do anything extra. The flowers could stay dead. She turned and looked back the length of the house, through the living room and kitchen, into the back room, where her red armchair sat with the rocker next to it, the chairs circling the now-cold wood stove. She was doing all this for the house, she thought, and decided to get dressed for work. Once dressed, she made the bed and walked through the house, straightening furniture, putting books and magazines in neat piles. She washed out her coffeecup and the coffeepot, she closed the windows in case it rained while she was away. The noise from the machines came through the closed windows and Arla felt how much she didn't want to go to work. If she could do something, not extra but unexpected, if she could do one bold thing, perhaps everything would change and grow easier. The glass house, she thought. The glass house was the way out. She would keep her job and part with Joseph, if only she could lay hands on the house. She looked at the length of her house again as if it were the length of her days. It didn't seem worth it to do anything anymore. She could not imagine waking anymore and going to work. She could not imagine another winter.

And she couldn't imagine Joseph dying so young. It didn't seem to her, any more than with her mother, that he was the kind of person to contract a mortal disease. Both of them were too rooted in daily things—he in his stages of building, she in deciding things for Arla. Arla saw her mother with the dolls

in the empty apartment, deciding to leave them there. She
wondered if anyone else adopted the dolls or if they were destroyed in the end. She could see Joseph in another future.
She could see him in a Christmas card, a series of Christmas-
card photographs of himself and his wife and children, despite
his liking for hotels. She would not be the wife, ever, his
disease or no, and now she saw how little she was to him. She
could do no more for him than for her mother. She was
speechless when speeches might help, but what could she
have said to either of them and what could she have done?
Both of them crawled into themselves and left her, gave her
no hints of what to do for them besides leave them as alone as
herself. If there was an extra gesture to make, an act to per-
form that would compensate for their loss and her helpless-
ness—she couldn't think about it. Her arms felt weak, as if
she would never lift anything again. Maybe the extra act was
to leave everyone alone.

She walked to the phone and dialed the Untereckers' number. This time the phone rang four times and a woman's voice
answered, which startled Arla: "Hello?"

"Mrs. Unterecker? This is Arla Stein of the Martin Collection. I've written you several letters about your glass house."
There was a long silence, and Arla felt like crying or hanging
up. She would start crying eventually, but it shouldn't be on
the phone with Mrs. Unterecker. She said again: "Hello?"

"This isn't Mrs. Unterecker," said the voice.

"I'm sorry. Do I have the wrong number?"

"No. You have the right number. The Untereckers are out."

"I wonder if they'll be at home later today. I'd like to come
and take a look at their glass house. I'll be in Montpelier anyway."

"If she said you could come look at the thing, come."

"I could be there around noon. If that's convenient."

"Suit yourself," the voice said. Arla took down instructions
from Montpelier to the Untereckers' house. When she hung
up, she didn't feel like crying anymore. Mrs. Unterecker never
had said she could come up. She'd never answered Arla's sec-

ond letter. Still, she would go. She thought of calling Bob to
say she wouldn't be in all day, but she shrugged in the manner
of Monique and decided not even to call. She liked the idea
that no one would know where she was or what she was
doing, if only for one day. Arla checked all the windows in the
house again to be sure they were closed. She took a sweater
with her, for it would be colder up north; then Arla left her
house. Once in the car, she thought of going back to check—
had she turned off the gas stove, had she closed all the doors?
Instead, she started the car and made her way slowly down the
road, over the bumps and the ridges, past the machines. One
of the men working waved to her, and she waved back. Then
she was off down the road, the house no longer in sight.

Arla drove through town, then out along the Battenkill
River to Vermont. In Arlington she turned north toward
Manchester. The route she knew took her across the mountains at Manchester Depot; then up 91, the new highway, then
Montpelier. The day was bright, and as she drove past the
large white buildings of Manchester—courthouse, hotel, mansion—Arla thought about summer. She thought of other places
she had been in the summer—New York, Boston—and of
cities in summer, with sun and traffic, fountains and plazas;
then she snapped her attention back where it belonged, on the
road. The mountain route at Manchester Depot passed several ski areas, and the lifts could be seen now, stopped for the
summer, waiting for the winter, wires against the now green
mountains. Only at the tops were patches of snow still evident. All along the road she saw houses and restaurants,
motels and hotels, all smartened up for tourists, then stretches
of cool woods, then more ski business. She pulled off the road
opposite an alpine lodge which flew flags of Canada and
America, France and Germany, and she looked at the map to
be sure she was going where she wanted. The local roads
ambled more gradually to 89, the road to Montpelier, but she
wanted to take the new highway. She had enough ahead of
houses and towns and motels and restaurants, the architecture
of the road. Arla continued on her way.

She had forgotten this sensation of the road. All the years in her house and in the museum, Arla had fought leaving, and when she left, fought to return. Now the road was the only place she wanted to be, the only place she could be. She loved the road and had forgotten it. On the road, no one knew her, and on the road, she owned nothing. Along the road, she passed houses she might have lived in, but she was free of stopping, looking, staying. She said to herself: I'm up to here with houses. She passed houses by, still thinking—bad window, unfortunate addition—but she passed them by. Yards past, they were forgotten and she didn't look back to check on them. She looked instead at the road, then her odometer and her watch. The road was coming at her and going through her, and with each mile covered, Arla felt more open and clean, and the road was more like the wind to her.

She hesitated at gardens. Little more than a week to Memorial Day, Vermonters had their gardens turned over, their peas planted, and they waited for the day to arrive when they would plant their starts, set out geraniums and petunias on their front porches. Flags waiting for Memorial Day waved to Arla, but she went on. Just before her road joined 91, she pulled to the side again and looked at the map. She saw it as a drawing, like Joseph's drawings, the lines signifying roads and towns, parks and mountains—all details she didn't care about. Good. She was covering distance, making time, and soon she would be on a road that was only a road.

Almost caught by the last house: it lay at the end of a stone path extending from road to house. There were good details: fretwork, twelve-over-twelve window—but Arla drove past, past houses, past houses and lawns, past flags and gardens. She entered the highway and it felt as if she were seeing the ocean again, trapped inland too long. The horizon had lifted at last. Everything was open, and the road was wide. The road was high, and over the edge were the valleys spreading below. She listened to the sounds of the engine and the wheels and the wind. She saw the sun, yet she was far from the sun. She was in the north and could have been imagining this world. She sat back and steered and thought of glass. From sand to fluid to rigid transparency, glass would occupy the museum and take the space. The glass wing—subtle steel structure, stronger than glass—would be transparent. Wall through wall, object through object; the only thing not transparent would be the people. The sun could melt the wing and melt the objects in the wing. What could be done to get rid of the people?

Montpelier at last. The golden dome on the state building shone in the midday sun. On the highest hill lay the last snow. Monique would laugh at this golden dome. Arla continued through town and noticed a pizza parlor, a Grand Union, stores identical to the stores where she lived. Following the directions she'd received on the phone, Arla drove several miles out of town. She passed this landmark and that—a turn in the road, a covered bridge—took a left and a right until she was out in the country. The landscape was cold in Montpelier, a spring cold, hanging on beyond its time and weakening, warm air seeping in through its cracks. The cold was the way it had been in April at home, and Arla thought perhaps she'd broken time barriers on her drive northeast, traveled to the weeks before when she didn't know what she knew now, when the road was the same and Joseph was whole. She saw a small country church, modest as a schoolhouse, another landmark in the instructions. If she kept going north, perhaps she would reach her childhood, but how would she know when to stop? Opposite the church a row of six mailboxes sat on posts, and on one of the boxes was painted the name UNTERECKER in white paint, a dribble falling forever from the second *e*. Just before the church, Arla turned onto a dirt road and drove until she came to the third house on the right. Opposite the house was what appeared to be a frozen lake. Arla thought of the futility of throwing herself into such a lake, trying to reach clear water below. She saw vegetation around the edges and in the center of the ice. The swamp was melting with spring.

Up a sharp incline on her right was a standard tract house that could have been anywhere. Its siding was pale green, and one picture window overlooked the icy swamp. Though the house looked several years old, it hadn't yet been landscaped. Mounds of dirt from the original excavation lay a few feet from the concrete-block foundation. There was one door at ground level facing the swamp, and another on the side of the house visible from the road. Pines from the surrounding forest leaned toward the house, and a snow shovel rested against the upper door, looking tired in the spotty sunshine. Arla wondered why anyone chose to live there. She drove up the driveway and parked her car at the other side of the house alongside a red convertible that had seen better days. She left her car and listened for some sound of human life, but there was none. Arla walked from her car to another, closer door that faced the woods. The door was half-glass, the glass covered on the inside by a red-and-white-checkered curtain. She could see rough forms through the curtain but couldn't distinguish what the forms were.

Arla knocked at the door and waited. On her watch it was noon, exactly when she'd said she would arrive. She knocked again, this time a little louder. The only public telephone she'd noticed was all the way back in town. She knocked again after an interval and decided she would wait another five minutes. She was getting cold in the shadows of the pines. As she was about to leave, she heard a sound from inside, and so she knocked again and waited a little longer. This time she heard footsteps and the door opened. At first she could not tell if the person standing before her was a man or a woman. On second glance she saw that the figure was heavily bearded. A red bandanna was wrapped around his head and he wore a faded embroidered shirt underneath huge overalls. He was a large man and occupied almost the whole of the doorway, height and breadth.

"Yes," he said in a voice light for his size. "Can I be of service to you?"

"I'm Arla Stein. I called this morning. And wrote. I'm from

the Martin Collection and I've come about the glass house. Professor Unterecker?"

"Now, use your eyes," the man said. "You wanted to come look. Do I look to you like a professor?"

Arla put out her hand to lean against the house. The sun had moved, and she used her other hand to shade her vision. In that posture, she felt she was blocking the doorway, though this man could have pushed her aside with a breath. She was weak now and remembered she was hungry. She hadn't eaten all day, and she felt hot from the sun in her eyes, cold from the pines. "Professors look like all kinds of people. Please. If you aren't Professor Unterecker, who are you?"

"I'm a houseguest of Mrs. Unterecker's. A cousin. Bosco Goldfarb. Want to come inside?"

The floor was linoleum, the color of dust. Arla could see nail marks protruding from the thin spackling job on the Sheetrocked walls. The walls were painted the same green as the outside of the house. To her right, Arla could see a living room. A card table stood at one end of the small room and at the other a single bed with a wrinkled madras spread and some pillows thrown casually over the spread. On her left was another room, almost dark. Arla could just see the foot of a bed and some lumpy bedclothes.

In back of Bosco was a stairway. He stepped aside and gestured for her to go ahead; she descended and he followed. Bosco had a sweet odor, or maybe it was the house. Down on the cellar level were two rooms, on one side a kitchen with a small refrigerator, a corner sink, and an apartment-size stove. The windows were set up high at the level of Arla's shoulders. The other part of the cellar was unfinished, with foil-backed insulation stapled between the studs. There was no flooring on that side, and the kitchen smelled damp from the dirt.

"Have they lived here long?" Arla asked.

"A few years. No one's here now," he said. "Charlene would love you to see the house, but today isn't a very good time."

"I should have come another day."

"That still wouldn't do much good. Charlene will be away for a while, and she won't let the house be seen unless she's here."

"Perhaps if Professor Unterecker were here," said Arla, "he would show me the house."

"It's his pride and joy. But he isn't here either. Cup of tea?"

Bosco boiled water in a topless aluminum coffee percolator and poured the water into a mug that looked as if it came from a diner. Then he floated a tea bag on the water and handed the cup to Arla. The tea was too hot to drink, the cup too hot to hold. Arla blew on the steam. If Bosco was an unlikely curator, this house was a more unlikely spot for a fragile object. She wondered if she was safe with him but didn't see what she could do about it. "Maybe I could look at it just for a moment," she said. "I'm experienced with art objects, all kinds. The house is here, isn't it?"

"It never leaves," Bosco said. "Charlene's grandfather had it made especially. He lived just up the road. And the last time it moved was when Charlene moved into this house. And that's that. We've had offers before."

"Perhaps later in the day," she said.

"Not very possible," Bosco said. "I'm sorry for your trouble, but this just isn't the time."

They sat in a silence that lasted until Arla burned her tongue on the tea. She gave up and thanked him for the tea, meaning to ask once more to see the house but not having the heart to be refused again. Bosco stood in the upper doorway as Arla got into her car. There was no room to turn around, and she had to back down the steep driveway. She drove past the church and the mailboxes, through town to the pizza parlor. She ordered a small plain pizza, coffee, and an apple fritter. Arla stood at the counter waiting for the pizza and the fritter to emerge from the oven, paid for the food, then carried her tray to a table by the window. She wondered if she would be better off if a friend were there, someone to tell everything to, but she wanted to accomplish something and telling would set her back. Arla remembered that when her mother died, she told as few people at boarding school as possible. It was a small place and everyone found out for themselves, but until she told someone herself, her mother remained alive in relation to that person. She ate the pizza and the apple fritter, drank the coffee, and went back to her car.

Arla drove past the Unterecker house to check that the red convertible was still there. There had been a slick on the surface of the tea Bosco Goldfarb served her, and she tasted soap despite the pizza, fritter, and coffee. The convertible was there. She drove as far as she could up the road, passing two other houses, older and larger than the Untereckers', and she discovered that the Untereckers' road, like her own, was a dead end. She traveled back down the road and decided to wait at the church for Bosco. He would probably come out eventually, and perhaps he could be persuaded to change his mind if he saw how persistent she was and how important the glass house was to her. She parked the car in front of the church where it was concealed from the road by a picket fence. Arla thought of getting out but remained in the car. The windows of the church were shuttered, and she wondered if the church was ever used. The house and road seemed like the end of the world. There was a small graveyard in the field near the mailboxes, but Arla didn't see any recent gravestones. All looked old-fashioned and weathered. She was thinking she should park where Bosco could see her, when the red convertible suddenly appeared and went right by her. She saw the red bandanna on Bosco's head; then the car was gone, and it was too late to signal to him. She started the car, intending to follow Bosco, but once the car was moving, Arla turned up the dirt road that led to the Untereckers' house.

The door wasn't locked. She went inside quickly, closing the door behind her and blocking the sound of the wind in the pines. Arla stood and listened. The only sound inside the house was the ticking of a clock and the click of the refrigerator downstairs. She began to look for the glass house.

In the living room there was a closet that held nothing but two metal folding chairs and a tennis racket. The bedroom was more formidable to search. It held an opaque darkness that Arla didn't want to enter. She found the light switch on the wall and surveyed the room. A lump of pajamas lay on the floor, and a sheer pink nightgown was bunched up next to it. The large bed was unmade, the café curtains held together with wooden clothespins. There was nothing hanging in the double closet but two wire hangers. All the clothing was piled on the floor. Arla thought it was possible that the glass house was concealed beneath the clothing, but she decided to look for it downstairs.

In the kitchen, her cup of tea and Bosco's rested side by side on the table. There were no cabinets in the kitchen, only open shelves filled with food—tuna fish and beans, SpaghettiOs and soup. Everything was in a can or a glass jar except one box of crackers. Surrounding the box were scattered crumbs and other evidence of mice. Arla moved on to the storage area. The glass house had to be there or upstairs in the bedroom closet. This was not the kind of house that had hiding places.

An old Schwinn lay on the dirt floor, a wheel tilted toward the ceiling. In one corner there was a collection of open paint cans and a wooden box with wads of steel wool and the encrusted handles of paintbrushes peeking over the edges. Next to the box Arla saw an object wrapped a little carefully, tucked away a little neatly, and she went to it. An old patchwork quilt, its stuffing coming through the weak spots, was tucked around the object. It was not a large object, no broader than a typewriter or a large punchbowl, about two feet high. She took the bundle in her arms and carried it from the damp-smelling storage space into the kitchen. There she set it down on the table, and, carefully as she knew how, Arla removed the quilt.

The glass house was three stories tall, a turreted and towered Victorian house, narrow, as if built to fit a certain space on a glass block. When Arla looked clear from the front door to the back, her eye passing through parlor and fireplace, back hall and kitchen, she saw only the transparent walls, not what was within them. Then she admired the detailing of the molding along the walls and the small pieces of furniture set on the glass floors—a table with delicate claw-and-ball feet, a footstool with immobile glass tassels hanging from its edges. There were no glass people in the glass house. It stood neat and trim, empty and expectant as a hotel room. The walls held prisoner the space inside. The outside walls were molded with a Gothic-patterned siding through which it was possible to see. The walls, inside and out, were a net over the house. On the dining-room wall Arla noticed a crack. It derived from a flaw in the glass. She bent over to see it, a microscopic bubble and a hairline crack that curved up to the ceiling of the dining room. Above the dining room was the master bedroom, and Arla looked down through the ceiling to trace the tiny flaw making its way across the room. It was the only thing moving in the glass house.

Arla heard a sound outside. A car passed by, neighbors up the road perhaps. She knew she had to leave. Where were the Untereckers, where was Bosco? It didn't matter, because Arla made a decision. She would take the glass house with her. She didn't have to think at all. The house would be safe with her, cared for properly, not stored with broken bicycles and used paintbrushes. It would be difficult to show a piece that had been stolen, but Monique with her money and power might find a way around that. In any case, it would be better off with Arla. Arla rewrapped the house in the quilt and carried it up the stairs. She balanced it on one arm as she opened the door. The glass house was awkward to carry, its protrusions fragile and incomprehensible underneath the quilt. She set the bundle on the floor of the car in back of the driver's seat; then she got into her car and drove off down the dirt road. Back to Montpelier, past the pizza parlor, through traffic lights, past the dome of the state capitol, Arla looked for a red convertible but saw none. She drove as quickly as the speed limit allowed, straight to the highway, reversing her morning journey. At one point she thought she saw Joseph's Volvo, but knew it wasn't his.

When she reached the highway, she looked at her watch.

There was plenty of light left in the day, light until eight at night. The light was growing toward the summer solstice, Arla thought, and would go on doing so. Solstice reached, the light would begin receding until, again December, winter solstice would come. Where would she be for summer solstice, winter darkness? There was nothing strange in the path of the light, but Arla felt depressed to think of the light coming and going, so indifferent to her. Bright or dim, the light would travel through the glass house with no interference from solid matter. Air was another matter. Glass was a definite barrier to air. Inside glass rooms nothing stirs and it is clean and orderly. The bed is always made and there are no dropped socks, no dishes from the night before. There is only glass space, open, saying to the world: Look! It is all here, so obvious, nothing to hide! Arla rolled down her window a little to let in the afternoon air.

There was little traffic on the highway. It looked to Arla as if she were the only person traveling, the only person not working or seated with family, not playing baseball or plowing a field, not planting a garden. She alone moved through and past the towns and farms as if they were trees, fixed objects to which to bid farewell, for traveling is another way of saying good-bye and parting is never completed. She watched a hawk falling and rising, disappearing from her view, and thought of the homeless life of birds. She tried saying it aloud: *Good-bye* to Joseph. And *Good-bye* . . . But the word *Mother* was too hard to say. *Joseph* was easy, and she made the words into a song, rolling down the window a little more, feeling free to sing where no one could hear. *Good-bye.* She thought of opening the door, of letting in all the air possible, and at sixty miles an hour the air would get a fine free ride through the car and through her also. She thought of flying the car over the embankment, for the road was once more the high road. Below was the valley of farms and houses and factories —all quiet, no smoke rising, no sign of life, only the wind going past her down the road.

Just before she reached the turnoff for Manchester Depot,

miles across the mountains, Arla rolled up her window. She felt tired. She had woken up early, she remembered, woken with Monique's call, and she hadn't slept right. She'd felt restless in her sleep, tired and restless as she felt now, wanting to stretch but finding no room. In sleep, what had held her back? A sign appeared for a rest area, and Arla slowed down, turned on her signal, and looked in the rearview mirror. There was no one behind her. At the rest stop there was nothing but a wire trash basket and a curved concrete wall. The area overlooked the valley. Arla parked the car at the center of the wall and turned off the engine. The only sound was the wind. She left the car and stood by the wall. There were hours to drive before she was home again, and then where would she be? She tried to think of what meat to defrost for dinner, of a salad she would make. She tried to think of something to want, but she couldn't. She didn't want to eat or drink. She wanted to sleep, but not yet. She thought of driving the glass house straight to the museum and leaving it there for Monique's arrival. If Bosco came after her at the museum—and there was no reason why he or the Untereckers couldn't find her there—Monique could stand him off or buy him off. Once Monique had her hands on the house, she would keep it as the Untereckers never could, under lock and key, under glass. Arla imagined the new wing with the glass house as its central display, on a glass pedestal designed for it by Joseph. Then she thought: No—for she saw herself nowhere in that glass picture or in that museum, and she knew that Monique would never use her money and her power to save Arla, only to save herself. Arla would keep the glass house for herself. She would carry the glass house upstairs in her own house, keep it there in the plaster dust, no walls, no ceiling, hide it there for the years it would take to acquire the money to complete her house. It would remain a secret. No one went upstairs without her, after all, and the new roof wouldn't bring any carpenters inside. Yet the glass house resting in her rooms would define the house forever. If she did find the money to finish the house, she would have to hide the house in a better place. The

barn was unsafe for the glass house; so were the garage and
the chicken house. There were no hiding places. She could
bury it, but what would the earth do to the glass? She regretted she had ever seen the glass house, regretted more that
she had taken it. It was too finicky and fragile to keep and
protect. Perhaps Mrs. Unterecker kept it in the dirt-floor
storage space wrapped in an old quilt because there was no
other place for a glass burden but tucked away safe from
everything, even from sight. Arla thought that perhaps she
had been tricked into taking the house, and perhaps at that
moment Bosco was celebrating that the burden was off them
forever and on to Arla. She looked up the highway for his car,
but nothing came along her way.

She considered returning the house. Aside from the difficulty of explaining the theft, she felt a reluctance to travel in
that same direction again, to go where she had been. What
she wanted was to divest herself of the glass house. Could
Bosco have guessed she would take it when she didn't know
herself? Why had he ever let her into the house? If she was
wrong and he wanted it back, there was no way to hide from
Bosco. It was too lonely on those northern roads, too hard to
keep going along the same roads. She would find a place for
the house, then a place for herself, for Arla wanted out. She
wanted to move, to be traveling again, and where didn't
matter.

She lifted the glass house from the back of her car and set it
gently on the ground. She took off the quilt and stepped back
a foot or so. Something had happened to the house. Perhaps
it was only the movement of her car during the ride down the
Untereckers' road or the stop at a light in Montpelier. Anything could have done it. The crack had widened, and her perfect record for the care of objects was broken. It was not bad
or fatal. There was not yet a fissure in the glass barrier between dining room and master bedroom, but Arla knew the
break was inevitable. There in the afternoon sunlight, sitting
on that nest of ragged quilt, the house caught the sun and sent
it back to the sky like a shot, refracted, fractured, the crack

breaking the light, as eventually the air would break through the glass surface. The house was broken and it was her fault. If she had left it where it was, it would have rested there forever, or until the quilt rotted from the dampness. But what did she care? For the years Arla had spent in Monique's museum and in her own house, for the care she'd given to walls and floors, to paintings and vases and sculpture, to entries in catalogs and footnotes in books, her care for dimensions in centimeters and inches, for provenance, medium, color, and date; for all the care, what did she care? And for Joseph, whom she might have cared for had she known him, to whom she might have said whatever word you say, or given him the touch of a hand now useless to her; what did she care for Joseph or he for her? Her mother, dead, came to her, sitting and rocking in the dark kitchen, in Arla's kitchen, crying and crying, and Arla knew now why her mother wept. She was in pain. She was afraid. She wept for herself, and nothing more. It was all herself, the things people did were for themselves. Arla had shut herself away and not hurt anyone, she had done everything right, created a quiet order to keep her moving smoothly through her life, but she had failed. She wanted nothing she had, not even the glass house.

Arla moved to the glass house and picked it up. It was lighter than a child, lighter than wet leaves in autumn. She raised it over her head and looked through the house to the wide sky and the road. Then she pushed the house down through the air with as much force as she had, and she watched the house break. It broke first into chunks, as if suffering an earthquake. The turret came off the right side, and the entranceway shattered. The parlor splintered, but its fireplace remained intact. Still the house looked like a house, so Arla stepped on the house until she had broken all the small pieces into smaller pieces still, and Arla walked on the house until there were no windows to see through and no doors, no floors, no ceilings, no siding, no walls, until there were no shards large enough for an archaeologist to name. She picked up the rag of a quilt and carried it over to the wall. She shook out the quilt, scattering the fractions of glass over the valley. Arla placed the quilt in the trash basket and moved things around—hamburger wrappers, wet newspapers, an empty oil can—until the quilt was hidden. Arla got back into her car. She was tempted to study the map to see where she was going, but she decided she could go just as well without one. She started the engine and drove away from the rest area without looking back. "The road," Arla said. "I love the road."